"He's an awful tall Indian," said Freddie

The Bobbsey Twins
At Pilgrim Rock

By

LAURA LEE HOPE

GROSSET & DUNLAP
Publishers   *New York*

Though this is a fictional story, the author has tried to present the historical Plymouth background accurately, including the present-day exhibits. Mr. Warren's museum and its contents are imaginary, however, as are the adventures of the Bobbsey Twins at Pilgrim Rock.

© Grosset & Dunlap 1956
All Rights Reserved
ISBN: 0-448-08050-8

Printed in the United States of America

The Bobbsey Twins at Pilgrim Rock

CONTENTS

THE BOBBSEY TWINS
AT PILGRIM ROCK

Grateful acknowledgment is extended by the author to Mr. Hubert Kinney Shaw, of Plymouth, and other descendants of the Pilgrims for their kindly assistance in providing historical data woven into this story.

CHAPTER I

SPOOKY NEWS

"HOW would you children like to take a trip and hunt for a ghost?" Mrs. Bobbsey asked, her eyes twinkling.

The two sets of twins, seated around the dining-room table, looked up from their luncheon.

"A ghost? You're teasing us!" exclaimed dark-haired Nan. She was twelve, like her brother Bert, a slender, happy-looking boy who sat beside her, grinning.

The younger twins, however, seemed serious. Freddie and Flossie, six years old and blond, gazed at their slim, pretty mother.

"A real ghost?" Freddie asked. "The kind that wears a white sheet?"

A smile came to Mrs. Bobbsey's lips. "I received a letter from Aunt Nan Shaw of Plymouth today," she explained. "Aunt Nan has asked us to come to Pilgrim Land to look for a ghost on Clark's Island. Besides, she has a surprise for you."

Mrs. Bobbsey had waited until the twins had nearly finished their meal of tomatoes stuffed with chicken salad before telling the exciting news.

Just then Dinah, the plump colored woman who helped Mrs. Bobbsey, appeared with a dish of cookies for dessert. "Did I hear somebody say ghosts?" she asked.

"We're going to find one," Flossie told her. "Aunt Nan knows where it is."

"You all had better be mighty careful," Dinah said with a wink as she set down the cookies. "And mind what Miss Aunt Nan tells you."

The children had not seen their mother's great-aunt for several years, but she was a favorite with them. In fact, Nan Bobbsey had been named for her.

"I wonder what the surprise is, Mother," Nan said.

Mrs. Bobbsey replied that their aunt had given no hint about this in the letter. "But I can guarantee it will be a good one," she added.

Bert eagerly asked, "Are we going to Plymouth?"

His mother smiled and nodded. "Dad and I have already talked it over. He'll accompany us as far as New York City where he has a business appointment. Then the rest of us will go on to Plymouth."

"Now I can see the place where the Pilgrims landed," said Nan.

"Me too." Flossie bobbed her head. "Is Aunt Nan a Pilgrim?"

"She's a descendant of one," Mrs. Bobbsey explained, saying that one of her great-aunt's ancestors was Edward Dotey, who came to America on the Pilgrims' ship, the "Mayflower."

"She can tell you all about it and show you points of interest," Mrs. Bobbsey continued, "And then there are many places to visit; for example, the miles of cranberry bogs."

"May we see them too?" Flossie asked.

Her mother said yes. "There's a small railroad at Edaville, which takes passengers all around the bogs, and they see how cranberries are grown."

"Goody, goody! I love cranberries," Freddie said. He jumped to his feet. "I want a cranberry sandwich right now. I'm hungry."

"But you just finished lunch," Nan reminded him.

"Please, may I have a cranberry sandwich?" Freddie asked his mother.

Mrs. Bobbsey laughed and said he might. There was a can of cranberries in the pantry.

"I'll open it," the little boy said. Flossie went

with him. Freddie climbed onto a stool and took the can from the pantry shelf. Climbing down, he inserted the top of the can into a can opener which hung on the wall.

Zip! Zip! The top of the can lifted out, showing luscious, red cranberry jelly.

"It's bee-yoo-ti-ful!" Flossie said, running to get a small dish.

Freddie tried to shake the cranberry jelly into the dish, but it would not come out. Suddenly Flossie remembered that Dinah sometimes opened both ends of a can. She suggested this to Freddie.

The boy cut out the bottom of it, but no sooner had he done this than the solid chunk of cranberry jelly began to slide out of the can with a gurgling sound.

Squoosh! It fell squarely on Freddie's white shirt. Quick as a flash, Flossie pushed a plate against her brother's belt buckle. The cranberry jelly landed with a *plop* on the plate.

"I saved it!" she cried out. "But look at you, Freddie!"

Hearing the commotion, Dinah hurried into the pantry. "Gracious sakes alive! What are you doing, Freddie?"

"He's making a cranberry sandwich out of himself," Flossie said, giggling.

Dinah quickly wet the end of a towel and

cleaned Freddie's shirt. Then she helped the children make cranberry sandwiches. They piled several on a plate and took them into the dining room.

"We're Pilgrims eating our first cranberries," said Bert. "Say, why don't we play The Landing of the Pilgrims at Plymouth Rock?"

He suggested that they use an old rowboat tied to the dock at their father's lumber yard, which was on the shore of Lake Metoka.

"We'll need more Pilgrims," Nan said. "Let's get our friends."

"I'll tell Charlie Mason and meet you all at the dock. But the boat won't hold more than six," Bert added.

He hopped on his bicycle and sped down the street to get Charlie, a good-looking, dark-haired boy who was also twelve. Bert's twin went to phone her friend, Nellie Parks, blond and pretty. Then Nan went for a bunch of old hat feathers and some ribbons. When she joined Freddie and Flossie, they asked her what the feathers were for.

"You'll see," she said. "Come on!"

Half an hour later the little crowd of children gathered at the dock. Bert stood in the rowboat.

"May I get in?" Flossie asked.

Nan told her that the first passengers to come ashore from the "Mayflower" in a small boat had been men. "Bert, suppose you, Freddie, and Charlie row out and be the first Pilgrims to land."

"But what'll *we* do?" Flossie wailed.

"We'll play Indian," Nan said. "We'll greet the Pilgrims when they land."

Bert pointed out a large rock some distance up the shore. "You Indians meet us there," he said, smiling. "Hop in, fellows."

Just then a boy of Bert's age raced across the dock, waving his arms and calling, "Wait! I want to play too."

"Oh phooey!" Freddie said. "It's Danny Rugg."

Danny was a young mischief-maker. He liked to bully smaller children. None of the "Pilgrims" wanted him to play, but they could not act mean about it.

"Okay," said Bert. "We're playing Pilgrims landing."

"Make room for me!" Danny demanded and jumped into the boat.

Freddie climbed over the seats to the bow while Danny and Charlie sat in the rear. Manning the oars, Bert pulled toward the rock.

Meanwhile, Nan had tied the ribbons around the girls' foreheads and stuck the feathers in them. Now the "Indians" ran along the shore and waited for the boys.

"Woo, woo, woo!" they shouted, clapping their hands back and forth over their mouths.

As the boys neared the rock, Freddie poised himself to step out.

"Hey, wait a minute!" Danny called. "I want to be the first Pilgrim to land."

"Let Freddie," Bert commanded.

"He's too small," Danny said, trying to push his way past Bert. They tussled. Suddenly Danny gave Bert a hard shove. The boy lost his balance and landed with a splash in the water. Danny snickered, jumped out of the boat, and ran off.

Meanwhile, Freddie shouted, "I've landed!"

"You're a good Pilgrim," Flossie told her twin.

Bert waded ashore. He was dripping wet, but his shirt and shorts dried quickly in the hot August sun.

"It's the girls' turn to be Pilgrims," Flossie announced.

They got into the boat, rowed out a distance, then returned to land. The boys gave Indian war whoops. Freddie especially liked this part of the game, but he made so much noise that Charlie said:

"Better pipe down, Freddie, or people in Lakeport will think there's a real Injun war!"

After the Bobbseys and their friends had played the game several times they took the boat

Bert lost his balance

back. Then they walked into the office of the lumber yard to see the twins' father. He was an athletic-looking man with a broad smile, and he chuckled sympathetically when he heard of the incident with Danny.

As it was nearly time for him to close the office, Bert asked if they might ride home with him in his station wagon.

"Yes," he replied. "But wouldn't you boys rather go with Sam? He's taking the small truck up to a neighbor's with some lumber."

Sam was Dinah's husband. The couple had an apartment on the third floor of the Bobbseys' large, rambling house and had worked for the family ever since the twins could remember.

"I'd like to ride in the truck," said Charlie, who did not often have this chance. Bert and Freddie sometimes went with Sam and helped him unload lumber, and they were happy to ride with him again that afternoon, so off they went.

Late that evening Mrs. Bobbsey said she thought it was time for her "Pilgrim" twins to get to bed.

"But it's so hot," Flossie spoke up.

"I have an idea," Nan said. "Mother, may we set up cots and sleep on the porch?"

At once the others begged her to say yes. "All right," she agreed.

Mr. Bobbsey and the boys brought the cots

from the garage, and Mrs. Bobbsey and the girls put sheets and light blankets on them.

When Freddie was ready, he said, "Please let Waggo sleep here too, Mother."

Mrs. Bobbsey thought this a good idea, so the fox terrier was brought in. Their big, shaggy dog Snap was left in the backyard kennel.

When the twins jumped into bed, their parents kissed them good night and went indoors.

The cot which Nan occupied was next to the porch railing. By lifting her head she could just peer over the bushes beside the porch. The noise of the crickets soon lulled all the children to sleep.

Nan did not know how long she had been dozing, when suddenly she was startled by a noise. Rising on one elbow, she glanced over the rail.

A ghost was staring at her!

CHAPTER II

AN UNWELCOME REQUEST

STARTLED by the ghostly figure, Nan screamed. The figure vanished as Bert jumped out of his cot.

"What happened?" he asked.

Nan pointed, her hand shaking. "Something white j-just looked in here!" she said.

Waggo began to bark, and Bert opened the screen door. "Get him, Waggo! Get him!" he called as the terrier dashed outside.

By this time Freddie and Flossie were awake, and Mr. Bobbsey was hurrying down the stairs. Bert and Nan followed Waggo.

Suddenly someone near the back fence cried out. Snap began to bark and Waggo growled. In a moment the terrier ran back to the Bobbseys dragging something white between his teeth.

Bert flipped on the back-porch light, and Nan bent down to take a white cloth from the dog's mouth. "It's a pillow case!" she gasped.

"Your ghost was wearing it, Nan," said Bert. "He must have had it over his head."

His twin agreed. "A joke, but an awfully scary one," she said.

Mr. Bobbsey had reached the children and wondered if the prowler had been bitten by Waggo.

"I don't think so," said Nan. "Waggo probably thought it was some kind of game and just tried to get the pillow case."

Bert and Mr. Bobbsey searched the bushes and garage, but no one was in sight.

"My guess is that the ghost was Danny Rugg," Bert said as they returned to the porch.

Mrs. Bobbsey, who had come downstairs, examined the pillow case carefully, but there were no identifying marks on it. "I doubt that the prankster will come back to get it," she said, "so somebody is lacking a good pillow case."

Everyone went back to bed, and Waggo lay at the foot of Nan's cot just in case the prowler should return. She was first to awaken next morning. When Bert roused, she said, "I know how we can find out whether Danny played that trick."

"How?"

Nan whispered something in her twin's ear, and Bert smiled. "Good idea, Nan! Let's try it!"

After breakfast Nan got the pillow case and whispered her plan to Dinah. "That's a mighty fine scheme, honey chile," Dinah replied, laughing heartily. "I'll do it right away, Nan."

The colored woman quickly washed the pillow case and ironed it. Then, after folding it neatly, she wrapped the case in brown paper. As she handed it to Nan, Dinah said:

"I sure hope you all don't have any more trouble with that Rugg boy before you go to Plymouth." Then the kindly woman whispered, "I hope your plan works."

Nan's eyes twinkled. "Come on, Bert, let's go!"

The two children hurried out of the house and walked several blocks until they came to Danny's home. They went up to the front door and rang the bell. Danny answered, a surprised look on his face.

"What do you want?" he asked.

"We'd like to see your mother," Nan answered politely.

"Yes, yes, who is it?" came Mrs. Rugg's voice impatiently from inside the house.

"It's the Bobbseys!" Danny said, scowling.

Mrs. Rugg came to the door and said, "If you're selling tickets, I can't buy any today."

"We're not selling anything," Bert said with a chuckle.

Nan smiled. "We have something for you, Mrs. Rugg," she said and offered her the brown package.

Danny looked from the Bobbseys to his mother and squirmed uneasily.

"Goodness, what is it?" Mrs. Rugg asked.

"Your missing pillow case!" Nan told her.

Danny's jaw dropped as his mother said, "Oh, thank you! I missed it from our clothesline last night. Where did you find it?"

She opened the package and identified the freshly ironed case as hers.

Bert told the story of the ghost. He did not mention Danny, but he kept looking at him.

Mrs. Rugg asked sternly of her son, "You got out of bed and went out late last night?"

Danny did not answer the question. "Waggo must have come here and pulled the pillow case off our clothesline!" he said.

"Sure," said Bert. "He can even jump up high and pull out clothespins!"

"Go to your room, Danny!" his mother ordered. Then she said to the twins, "Thank you for having the pillow case laundered."

"I have to get my bike off the curb," Danny told his mother. "The Bobbseys might snitch it," he added spitefully under his breath.

As the Bobbseys walked toward the street Danny followed them. Just then Waggo came trotting down the sidewalk. He jumped up to lick Bert's hand.

"Good boy," said Bert, glancing at Danny. "Found any more ghosts this morning?"

"Oh, you think you're smart, don't you?" Danny said, scowling. "Well, I'll get even with that mutt!" He bent over and picked up a stick lying near the curb. "Take that!" he cried and flung the stick at Waggo.

"*Yike! Yike!*" Waggo yelped and dashed to the protection of Nan's side.

"Danny, you're cruel and horrid!" she cried.

"You're not going to get away with this!" Bert cried. Doubling his fist, he hit the bully in the chest, spinning him around.

"I'll fight you!" Danny shouted. "And beat you! I can throw sticks if I want to!"

At first Danny seemed to be winning. He forced Bert to stagger backward under his pounding blows. But Bert suddenly delivered a good crack at Danny's mid-section. The boy howled and bent over, offering a perfect target for Bert's fist.

Whack! Bert jabbed him on the nose. The bully yelled and ran into the house, calling loudly for his mother. The twins, followed by Waggo, hurried home.

"Think of the fun we'll have at Plymouth without Danny around," Nan said as they went into their own house.

The Bobbseys always had fun together and often shared the excitement of solving little mysteries. Their latest adventure had taken place aboard Their Own Little Ferryboat!

Nothing was heard of Danny that afternoon while the Bobbseys prepared for their trip. The twins helped pack. Freddie and Flossie had been given permission to take some small toys.

"I'm going to pack two little twin dolls in a special suitcase," said Flossie. "There'll be room for a couple of their extra dresses."

"I think I'll take my brief case," Freddie said importantly. He had received a miniature one for Christmas. In it he kept cutouts of fire engines from newspapers and magazines.

As Flossie packed, she said, "Freddie, what do you suppose Aunt Nan's surprise will be?"

Freddie sat down on the floor and thought. "Probably something to do with Pilgrims."

This idea pleased his sister. "Oh, I'd love to be a Pilgrim," she said. "They wore such pretty costumes."

The dinner table conversation was occupied mostly with talk about the early days of America. Mr. Bobbsey told of an Indian, Squanto, who had been captured by English sailors several years before the Pilgrims came to America. He had been taken across the ocean to London. There he learned to speak English.

"And didn't he ever see his Indian friends again?" Flossie asked, worried.

"Oh, yes. Squanto was returned to his Indian friends. And when the Pilgrims landed in Plymouth on December 21, 1620, how surprised they were to find an Indian who could speak their language!"

The twins' father related how Squanto taught the Pilgrim fathers to put fishes in each hill of corn they planted to make the corn grow better.

As he finished the story, the telephone rang. Nan answered. She came back to say, "It's for you, Mother. It's Mrs. Rugg!"

"Oh-oh," Bert said as Mrs. Bobbsey left the room. "She's complaining about me, I'll bet."

After Mrs. Bobbsey came back to the table, Nan said quickly, "Is she angry at Bert?"

"No," Mrs. Bobbsey said, half smiling.

"What did she say?" Nan asked.

Her mother sighed as she said, "Mrs. Rugg wants us to take Danny to Plymouth with us!"

CHAPTER III

"HOLD THE TRAIN!"

"MOTHER, you didn't promise Mrs. Rugg we'd take Danny with us!" Nan groaned.

"Now don't worry, dear." Mrs. Bobbsey explained that Danny would not be with them during their entire vacation. "He and Mrs. Rugg are going to New York, then to Boston. While she is visiting her sister in Boston, Danny will go to Plymouth to stay with some friends named Rench. They have a son Danny's age whom he will play with. Mrs. Rugg merely wants me to take him from Boston to Plymouth."

"Oh, I hope he behaves!" Flossie put in.

"I doubt it," Bert said wryly. "Say, is he going to New York and Boston on the same train we are?"

When Mrs. Bobbsey nodded, all the twins groaned, and Freddie said, "Danny will probably do something to make the train go backward."

The others laughed, and Mr. Bobbsey said, "I hope not or you'll be back home before you start."

Forgetting Danny for the next hour, the twins discussed the trip. They were thrilled to learn that they were going on a sleeper.

"Remember the time we were on a train and ate a sandwich five miles long?" Flossie said, giggling. It had taken her that distance to finish eating it.

"May I sleep upstairs in the train?" Freddie asked his mother.

She hugged him. "You mean the upper berth. All right, you can climb the ladder. Bert can sleep in the lower berth below you."

The twins went to bed happy and woke up the next morning wishing evening would hurry and arrive. Finally it was time to leave the house.

Dinah promised to take good care of Waggo, Snap, and Snoop, the Bobbseys' cat, while the family was away. When the Bobbseys and their luggage were in the car, they waved good-by to her. Sam drove them to the railroad station. Danny Rugg and his mother were already there, and they all boarded the train for New York.

Nan and Flossie shared a lower berth. Soon all the twins were fast asleep. When they awoke the train was nearing New York City. By the time the Bobbseys had dressed and eaten breakfast in the dining car, the train had gone underground into Grand Central Station.

"Here's where you change trains," said Mr. Bobbsey as the porter came to pick up their luggage. He said they would have a half-hour's wait. "I must hurry off right away," he told the twins. "You'll find the bags on the other train."

When they reached the big room where the ticket offices were, he said, "Have a good time with Aunt Nan."

"We will!" Freddie said. "And we'll find the ghost, too!"

The twins and their mother wandered into several shops in the station. Finally they came to a store which sold coloring books.

"Oh, look!" Flossie said. "There's a coloring book of Pilgrims. Please, may I have it?"

Mrs. Bobbsey bought it, and Freddie put it into the small brief case which he was carrying.

"May Nan and I look around by ourselves for a few minutes?" Bert asked.

"Yes, but don't forget the train to Boston is on track 10. I'll give you your tickets. Put them in your pockets. I'll meet you at the gate."

Bert and Nan walked about the station, intrigued by the huge pictures of trains on the walls.

Presently Bert took hold of his sister's arm. "Look! Here comes Danny!"

Their Lakeport neighbor hastened toward them, trying to manage a smile.

"Let's not bother with him," Nan urged in a low voice.

Danny, sensing this, ran toward them and said, "Come on, let's walk around together."

"No, thank you, Danny. You'll try to play a trick on us," said Nan.

"Not this time," Danny promised. "We'll have some real fun. How about it?"

"Oh, all right."

The three children wandered about, gazing at the travelers hustling through the station. Presently Bert said, "It's nearly time for our train to leave. Wasn't it on track 10, Nan?"

"It's on track 2," Danny told him.

"I thought Mother said track 10," Bert replied, wondering whether he had heard her incorrectly.

But Danny insisted that the train to Boston was on track 2. "If you go to track 10," he said, "you'll miss the train."

Bert and Nan asked Danny if he was sure of his information, and the boy nodded his head vigorously. "That's where I'm going—to track 2," he said.

Thinking he must be right, Bert and Nan headed for the gate with a big white 2 above it.

The time of departure listed was theirs. Danny trailed behind them.

Other people were hurrying to the gate, so the Bobbsey twins increased their speed. They had to wait in line for others to go through the gate before them.

Suddenly Bert looked up at the names of stations posted below the time. "Nan, it doesn't say Boston. And Danny's gone," he exclaimed.

"Let's ask the trainman at the gate," said Nan nervously.

It was three minutes before departure time as they came to the trainman at the gate.

"Does this go to Boston?" Bert asked.

"You have the wrong track," the man replied. "The train to Boston is on track 10. You'd better hurry, or you'll miss it!"

Nan grew pale. Suppose the train should start without them!

Bert grabbed his sister's hand and they raced toward gate number 10.

"Oh, I'm afraid we're going to be too late!" Nan wailed as they saw the attendant about to slam the gate shut. "And where's Mother?"

"Wait—wait for us!" Bert cried out.

The uniformed man pulled a watch from his vest pocket and glanced at it. He spoke to someone inside the gate.

"Hurry!" he called. "You kids ought to pay more attention to the time."

Bert and Nan squeezed through the gate. *Bang!* It shut after them. Mrs. Bobbsey and the small twins were standing on the platform, looking up and down frantically. Together they hurried along and stepped into their car just before the conductor gave the signal to the engineer to start the train.

"Danny tricked us again!" Bert said hotly, provoked at himself for believing the boy.

"We'll never believe him again," Nan said. When they found their seats, she told Mrs. Bobbsey the reason they were late.

"I guess playing mean tricks is part of Danny's nature," Mrs. Bobbsey said, shaking her head.

In the meantime Bert had noticed Danny sitting alone a few seats ahead. His mother was talking to the conductor at the end of the car. Danny's shoulders were shaking with mirth.

Bert walked up to him. "Why did you tell us the wrong train?" he demanded.

"I told you track number 10," Danny said.

Bert clenched his fist. "Oh, could I punch you!" he whispered. "I'll take care of you later."

By now the train was out of the underground maze of tracks and was heading out of the city.

"Hurrah! We're on our way to see the ghost!"

Freddie shouted, and the passengers about him looked puzzled.

Bert and Nan busied themselves looking at magazines while Freddie and Flossie worked on the coloring book. Finally they tired of this and asked their mother if they might go to the end of the car for a drink of water.

When she said yes, the small twins, holding hands, walked to the rear of the coach. But they could not get any water from the cooler.

"I guess it's empty," said Freddie. "Let's see if there's any in the next car, Flossie."

It was hard for him to open the door, but with Flossie's help he managed it. The little twins entered the car behind. Still they could not get any water. They kept going from car to car.

Finally they came to the last coach. There were only two people in it. One of them was a tall, sandy-haired man with a scar on his left cheek. He sat straight up in his seat, holding a black bag on his lap. As the children passed him, the train lurched, and Freddie bumped against him.

"Watch what you're doing!" the man said, glaring at the little boy.

"I—I'm sorry," said Freddie. "I didn't mean to bump into you."

"You nearly broke some valuable things in my bag," the man grumbled.

Looking sheepish, Freddie continued on with his sister until they came to the door at the end of the car. They gazed down the tracks stretching out behind them like a long snake.

Suddenly the twins heard a voice behind them. They turned to see Danny Rugg.

"Want to go out on the rear platform?" he asked them.

At first the younger children were hesitant to

go, but finally Freddie said, "Yes, if you'll go with us."

Danny opened the door, and the three walked out. There was only a small platform here, with nothing between the children and the flying tracks but a small metal gate.

"Oh, look what's here!" Danny said, glancing down at the platform.

At one side stood two trainmen's lanterns. Around one lantern hung several long red tubes which looked like firecrackers. On the other were little square brown things which Flossie said reminded her of cookies.

"What are they?" Freddie asked Danny, shouting to be heard. Danny shrugged.

Just then the car rounded a sharp curve and lurched. Flossie and Freddie were thrown first to one side of the platform, then to the other.

Danny ducked inside the train as it reached another curve. The little twins clung to each other, fear in their eyes.

Suddenly the train lurched again. The children were thrown against the back gate!

CHAPTER IV

MISSING TORPEDOES

"OW!" Flossie Bobbsey cried out as she and Freddie banged into the gate of the speeding train.

They were fearful that the gate might fly open. Freddie, holding his twin's hand, tried to get to the door but almost fell down. Just then the door opened and the conductor stepped out. He quickly reached for the two children and led them inside the coach.

"You had no business out there," he said, looking at them sternly. "Where are your seats?"

When Freddie told him, the conductor took the twins back to their mother. She was amazed to hear they had been found on the back platform. "Goodness, I thought the rear door was always kept locked!" she said.

The conductor declared that this was usually the case, especially when children were aboard the train. But since there had been only two adults in the last car, he had failed to take the precaution.

"Anyhow, they're safe," he said, smiling, "even though they're kind of mussed up."

"Danny was a meanie to leave us all alone," said Flossie.

"Who is he?" the conductor asked, interested.

Freddie pointed him out. "He's a trick-playing meanie," the little boy said.

Bert and Nan took the younger twins off to wash and comb their hair. When they came back, Freddie said he was hungry.

Mrs. Bobbsey glanced at her wrist watch. "I guess it is time for lunch," she said. "The dining car opens at twelve. We'll go and eat."

After the headwaiter had shown them to seats, Flossie looked up at him and said, "We're going to Pilgrim Land, so I'd like a Pilgrim sandwich, please."

"Just what is that?" the man asked.

"A cranberry jelly sandwich," Flossie told him.

The waiter laughed and said she might have it. "And would you like a little Thanksgiving turkey to go with it?" he asked.

"Yes, please."

This sounded so good that the other Bobbseys ordered it too. To their surprise the bread was toasted slightly and the slice of turkey in each sandwich was warm.

"Yummy, this is wonderful," said Nan.

"Mmm," Freddie added. "The Pilgrims sure knew how to eat!"

The sandwiches were followed by dishes of vanilla ice cream with fresh peaches on top. The meal ended with a lollipop for each child.

The twins were very happy as they walked back to their seats. They wondered why the conductor, who stood waiting for them, had such a stern look on his face.

"Is something wrong?" Mrs. Bobbsey asked him, seeing that the man was evidently disturbed about something.

"Six fusees and three torpedoes are missing from one of my lanterns on the rear platform. They're very dangerous in the hands of children."

"We didn't take any," Freddie spoke up.

The conductor said that Danny Rugg and the small twins had been the only ones on the train who had gone out on the rear platform.

"I've spoken to the Rugg boy. He denies taking either the fusees or the torpedoes. He suggested that perhaps Freddie and Flossie had."

Flossie burst into tears. "We didn't! We didn't!" she sobbed.

"There, there, don't cry," Mrs. Bobbsey said,

putting an arm around her small daughter. "If you say you didn't take them, we know you didn't."

"But—but the conductor thinks we did!"

"Well, I guess I was wrong," the man said. "I just wanted to make sure that you two didn't have such dangerous playthings in your pockets."

Bert whispered to Nan, "Do you suppose Danny took them?"

"I hope not, if they're dangerous."

The conductor was sorry he had upset the small twins so much. "Don't worry any more about it," he said.

Sitting down on the arm rest of the seat next to Freddie, he asked, "Have you children ever seen a fusee when it's lit?"

"No," they all answered.

The conductor told them that the fusee was used at night and made a big red light. "If the engineer sees one burning on the track," the conductor went on, "he knows he must stop his train for five minutes."

"Why?" Freddie asked.

The man said it was because the train in front had slowed down or was in trouble. The flare was a warning to the train behind so it would not bump into the one ahead.

"And what are the torpedoes used for?" Flossie asked. She had often heard them go *bang bang* on the railroad that ran through Lakeport, but never knew the reason for it.

The conductor said that the torpedoes, called "guns" by trainmen, were also put on the track as a warning. These were used a good deal in the daytime.

"So the back train won't catch up to the front one?" Flossie asked.

"Exactly," the conductor answered, smiling. Then he stood up. "Well, before we know it, we'll be in South Station, Boston. I have to get back on the job now."

After he left, the young twins discussed with their mother who could have taken the flares and the torpedoes.

"Maybe someone thought the torpedoes were cookies," Flossie suggested.

"I hope nobody tries to eat them!" said Bert, laughing. "He might stop the train!"

After a few more miles the conductor came into the car calling out, "Route 128."

"Is that a station?" Freddie asked, wrinkling his nose in perplexity.

Bert told him it was. The railroad crossed an important highway at this point.

Their train stopped to let people off, then continued on. Finally the conductor cried out:

"Boston. South Station, Boston."

"Hurrah, hurrah! We're almost to the ghost!" Flossie said, hurrying to pack away her dolls and coloring book.

Just as the train was stopping, Mrs. Rugg came to speak to the twins' mother. She wanted to make plans about Danny's going to Plymouth with the Bobbseys. The two women stepped off the train and continued chatting as they walked along the platform.

Danny and the twins trailed along behind, carrying their small luggage. All the children became interested in the hand trucks piled high with freight of all kinds.

"Oh, look, aren't they cute!" Nan said, pointing to a stack of flat cardboard boxes with holes along the sides. Several fluffy little heads peeked out.

"Baby chicks!" Freddie exclaimed.

Setting down their suitcases, the twins pushed close to the cardboard boxes to peer inside.

"Listen to the noise they're making!" Flossie said. "I wonder if that's because they're unhappy."

Nan told her that the baby chicks would soon be in their new homes.

"Ugh! What an awful noise they're making!" Danny said, stepping up. He pulled a long pencil from his pocket and poked it inside one of the holes.

Several fluffy little heads peeked out

"Don't do that! You'll hurt the baby chicks!" Nan cried out.

"Who cares!" Danny replied.

Nan looked about for her mother and Mrs. Rugg, but they were far up the tracks. Danny continued to poke at the chicks.

"Stop it, Danny!" Bert said as the cheeping became louder than ever.

Finally Bert gave Danny a shove, making him withdraw the sharp-pointed pencil.

The bully gave him a black look. "You can't push me around like that!" he said.

Suddenly Nan spied a big wooden box. One end of it was covered with screening, and inside were several dozen small rats.

"Look at these!" she called out, trying to divert Danny's attention.

Nan read the label and said, "The rats are being shipped to a medical laboratory. How interesting!"

But Danny Rugg was not interested. He was still angry about being pushed aside. "Who cares for a lot of rats?" he said, at the same time trying to give Bert a hard shove.

Bert did not want to have a fight in the station. He stepped aside nimbly. As he did, Danny's outstretched hand hit the box of rats.

"Look out!" Bert shouted as the box teetered off the top of the hand truck.

Danny tried to grab the falling box, but he was too late.

Crash! It landed on the platform pavement. One of the wooden sides broke open. The rats scurried out!

CHAPTER V

A MYSTERIOUS NOTEBOOK

SEVERAL travelers screamed and yelled as the rats ran across the station platform.

"Help me catch them, Danny!" Bert demanded. He bent down to grab one of the rodents, but it scurried away.

The boys, together with several men, did their best to capture the laboratory rats. But in spite of their efforts the animals scampered here and there.

Suddenly Bert spied a tall man wearing glasses and carrying a butterfly net. Bert ran up to him. "May I borrow your net for a moment, sir?" he asked.

Seeing the situation, the man handed over the net. *Swish! Swish!* Bert caught up several of the rats and put them back into the cage. Freddie held the board down so they would not escape again.

The commotion brought Mrs. Bobbsey and Mrs. Rugg running back to the scene. Behind them came the man in charge of freight. By this time Bert had caught all the rats that were in sight. But more than half of them could not be found. The freight man told Mrs. Rugg she would have to pay for the loss.

Danny was frightened. "It was an accident," he said. "I—I didn't mean to do it."

Nevertheless, Mrs. Rugg was angry. "I ought to punish you by not letting you go to Plymouth," she said.

"Oh, please! I'll be good!" Danny promised.

Finally his mother gave her consent. After the freight agent had taken her name and address, she said good-by to the others and hurried off.

Inside the station the twins' mother bought tickets for the ride to Plymouth. Twenty minutes later the Bobbseys, along with Danny, were seated in a two-coach Diesel train. It soon rumbled off in a southerly direction toward the historic old town.

"Bert, suppose you and Danny play checkers," Mrs. Bobbsey suggested.

As there were not many people in the railroad car Bert and Danny arranged two seats to face each other. Then, holding the checkerboard between them on their knees, the boys started to play. Bert won the first two games.

Danny took the third. After Bert won the next, Danny grumbled, "I've had enough of this old game."

"Okay, Danny." Bert folded the checkerboard and put the pieces back into a box.

Danny had reached into his shirt pocket and pulled out a small black notebook. He thumbed through several pages.

"Keeping a diary?" Bert asked him.

"Uh, uh," Danny said.

Bert could not help seeing the pages of the little black book. They had no writing on them. Noticing Bert's curiosity, Danny smirked and put the notebook back in his pocket.

He now reached up to the baggage rack over his head and pulled down a small suitcase he had been carrying. Opening it, he reached in for a bar of candy. Something else attracted Bert's attention. It looked like a fat, red colored pencil.

Bert immediately thought of the missing fusees. He said, "What's that red thing in your suitcase, Danny?"

The bully flushed and quickly snapped the suitcase shut. "Mind your own business," he said unpleasantly.

He pulled the wrapper from the candy bar, munched on it and said no more. He did not offer any of the candy to Bert.

Just before the train reached Plymouth, a man with a scar on his cheek arose from his seat and started down the aisle. He walked with bent knees and a long stride. His shoulders were hunched. In one hand he carried a round, black leather bag.

Freddie looked up from his coloring book and nudged his mother. "Here comes the man who scolded me for bumping into him on the way from New York," the boy said.

Nan, who was sitting opposite her mother, glanced toward the fellow. "He gives me the creeps," she whispered.

The twins were surprised when the man stopped at Mrs. Bobbsey's seat and bent over to speak to her. In a low, hoarse voice he said:

"You look like a person who would appreciate a real bargain, ma'am."

"Are you selling something?" Freddie piped up.

The man paid no attention to the boy's question. "I have some fine New England antiques. I must get rid of them for I need the money."

He started to open his bag, but Mrs. Bobbsey said, "Before you show me anything, I'd like to see your credentials."

The man shot an annoyed glance at her. "Credentials? What do you mean?" he demanded.

"I wouldn't buy antiques from a stranger,"

she said. "First I'd like to know who you are."

By this time the black bag was open far enough for Nan to glance inside. She could see a large pewter pitcher. But before her eyes could take in anything else, the man snapped the bag shut. With an angry look, he said, "I don't have to sell you my things. Lady, you've just missed a big bargain!"

With that he strolled down the aisle again and took his seat.

"I don't like him," Freddie said.

"He's scary, isn't he, Mother?" Flossie added.

"Well, yes. But people can't help looking the way they were born," Mrs. Bobbsey told her. "A homely person can have the most wonderful character you could wish for."

A little later the train pulled into the Plymouth station. Glancing out the windows to the left, the children could see the sparkling harbor.

Collecting their baggage, Danny and the Bobbseys stepped off the train. The moment Danny alighted he spied Mr. and Mrs. Rench and their son George.

"Hi!" he called. "Here I am! Let's go!"

Without bothering to say good-by or introduce the Bobbseys to his friends, Danny ducked off to their waiting car.

"I guess he doesn't know any better," Flossie whispered to Nan, tossing her head.

Just then a taxi drove up. The Bobbseys saw a handkerchief flutter from the rear window.

"There's Aunt Nan!" Mrs. Bobbsey exclaimed, as a sweet-faced, elderly woman stepped out.

"How are you, my dears?" Aunt Nan said. She and Mrs. Bobbsey exchanged affectionate hugs.

Freddie and Flossie flung their arms around their relative.

"Goodness, how you've grown!" she said, then kissed the older twins.

Aunt Nan was slender, and stood very straight for her age. Her hair was snow-white and wavy. She wore glasses which were attached by a small silver chain to a little button on the shoulder of her dress.

After the baggage had been stowed in the trunk of the taxi everyone climbed in.

"Where's the ghost hiding?" Freddie asked his aunt immediately.

"And what's the surprise you have for us?" said Flossie, who had wriggled into Aunt Nan's lap.

"I'll tell you the answers after you've seen Plymouth Rock," she said, laughing. "You know that's a custom of mine. You're not really part of Pilgrim Land until you've seen the rock."

It was not a long ride to Aunt Nan's house.

The taxi turned to the left into North Street and stopped halfway down the block.

"What a big place!" Nan remarked when they stood in the cool front hall of the lovely old-fashioned home. Aunt Nan explained that she rented some of the rooms to visitors. This gave her some extra income.

Mrs. Bobbsey was to share Aunt Nan's bedroom on the second floor. The twins were given two rooms on the third floor. Bert glanced out his window.

"Boy, the harbor looks keen!" he said to Freddie. "I see a lot of boats."

"Come on, let's hurry and look at Plymouth Rock," Freddie said. "Can you see it from here, Bert?"

"No. It's down on the waterfront."

After the Bobbseys had unpacked, they met in the spacious first-floor parlor.

"I do hope you'll have a wonderful vacation," Aunt Nan said. "And now, suppose you go look at Plymouth Rock while your mother and I talk."

She gave them the simple directions to the waterfront, and the children trooped down North Street. After they passed under the row of towering linden trees, the twins came to a breath-taking sight. They found themselves on a hill overlooking Plymouth Harbor. Motor cruis-

"That's Plymouth Rock down there,"

Freddie cried. "Let's look at it!"

ers and sailboats crisscrossed back and forth across the water.

Beneath them on the shore front was a tall granite portico. Under its canopy the twins could see a black iron railing.

"The rock's in there," Bert said, pointing down the grassy slope.

"This must be Cole's Hill that I've read about," Nan remarked. "Yes, it is, because there's the statue of Massasoit."

"Who was he?" Freddie asked.

"A fine Indian. He was a great sachem of the Wampanoags."

The other children glanced to their right. On top of a boulder stood the statue of a tall, handsome Indian. A knife was sheathed at his side, and in his left hand he held a peace pipe.

"He's an awful tall Indian," said Freddie. "Maybe ten feet."

The young twins ran over to gaze up at the statue. Nan looked around. Then she reminded Bert that it was on this hill that the Pilgrims had buried the people who died during the first winter they were in America.

"And wasn't grain planted over the graves so the Indians wouldn't know that only a few settlers were left?" Bert asked.

Nan nodded. "Those poor people," she said. "Weren't the Pilgrims brave, Bert?"

"They certainly were," he replied.

Freddie and Flossie by now had skipped back to join the older twins.

"Let's take a look at the rock now," Bert said. He started down the granite steps leading from the top of Cole's Hill.

"I'm going to run down on the grass," Freddie announced. "That's more fun."

"Me too," Flossie said. She took her brother's hand, and her blond curls blew in the breeze as she dashed down the hill with her twin.

But Freddie and Flossie ran so fast that they lost their balance. Plunging forward, they tumbled headfirst on the green slope. They rolled over and over toward the bottom!

CHAPTER VI

OVERBOARD!

BLUE sky, green grass, and the silver bay were a mixed-up blur to the small twins as they tumbled down Cole's Hill. When they reached the bottom, both were lying flat on their backs.

Looking up, they saw a smiling young man who helped them to their feet. He was dressed in green pantaloons and jacket. A large white collar and high-crowned black hat completed his costume.

Freddie blinked. "Am I seeing you in a dream, or are you a real Pilgrim?" he asked.

The young man laughed and replied, "I'm playing the part of a Pilgrim. I'm a guide to show visitors around. In a few minutes I'll tell a group about Plymouth Rock. Would you like to join us?"

"Oh, yes."

Bert and Nan, who had seen their brother and

sister tumble down the long hill, had raced for the steps and now arrived alongside the others.

"Are you both all right?" Nan asked as she brushed bits of grass and dirt from Flossie's dress.

"Sure," said Freddie. "And it was fun to get picked up by a Pilgrim."

He and Flossie took their brother's and sister's hands and went across the street to the beautiful granite portico covering Plymouth Rock.

When they came to the iron railing they looked down into a pit. "There it is!" Bert said, looking at the rock with the date, 1620, cut into its face.

"Huh, it's not so big as Danny Rugg told me," said Freddie. "He said it was high as a cliff!"

The guide remarked that many people had a wrong idea about the size of Plymouth Rock. He chuckled. "One man thought it would take all day to climb it!" he said, and the twins laughed.

The eastern side of the portico had an opening to the bay. Since it was high tide, water lapped about the base of the rock. By this time a group of sightseers had gathered.

"I'll tell you something of the history of the rock," he said.

The Bobbseys listened quietly. The guide said this was the exact spot where the Pilgrims had landed. "Later some men tried to drag the rock to the town square. But the upper part broke off."

"You mean they only had half a Pilgrim rock?" Flossie called out.

The guide smiled. "That was about it. One half stayed in the town square until 1888. Then it was carted back to the shore."

"And the top and bottom were put together again," Freddie guessed.

The guide said this was when the canopy was erected. "The present portico was given to the Commonwealth of Massachusetts in 1921 by the National Society of the Colonial Dames of America."

"Whew!" Freddie whispered to Nan. "That's a long name. But they must be nice ladies."

After the twins had viewed the rock from all sides, they thanked the guide.

"There are other places to visit here," the young man said, smiling. "Don't forget the first house and the old fort."

"We can't go anywhere else 'til Aunt Nan tells us about the ghost," Flossie told him. She tugged at her sister's hand. "Come on!"

The children hurried up the steps of Cole's Hill and ran back along North Street to Aunt Nan's house.

"Well, what did you think of Plymouth

Rock?" Aunt Nan asked as the children trooped into the parlor.

Nan answered first. "It's wonderful to think that the Pilgrims' first steppingstone in America is still here."

"And always will be," Bert added.

"It was swell," said Freddie.

Flossie nodded. "Now, what about the ghost, Aunt Nan? You promised."

"All right. I'll tell you."

The children seated themselves on the floor in front of her. She adjusted her spectacles firmly on her nose.

"There's said to be a ghost on Clark's Island," the elderly woman began. "It never hurts anybody, but the people there wish it would go away. So I thought you children might like to try to solve the mystery."

"Where is Clark's Island?" Bert asked.

Aunt Nan explained that the island lay in Plymouth Bay.

"The Pilgrims nearly settled there," she said. "It was named for Clark, first mate on the 'Mayflower.' He set foot on the island before anyone else." Aunt Nan smiled and blushed a little. "But he nearly didn't make it."

"How's that?" Bert asked.

"One of my ancestors pushed him out of the way," she replied.

The others laughed, and Nan asked who the person was. She had forgotten.

"Edward Dotey was his name. He wanted to step foot on the island first, but the other Pilgrims held him back and gave the honor to the first mate."

Aunt Nan explained that Clark's Island was privately owned, but she could arrange for the Bobbseys to go there.

"Let's find the ghost right away!" Bert urged.

"Wait a minute!" Nan interrupted. "What about the surprise you have for us, Aunt Nan?"

The old lady's eyes sparkled as she said, "How would you twins like to be in a Pilgrim parade?"

"Yippee! I love parades!" Freddie said.

"Will we march in costume?" Nan asked.

Their aunt said, "Yes. Every Friday during August the townspeople hold a Pilgrim's Progress."

She told them the actors in it played the part of the settlers who lived through the first winter. Led by a drummer, they marched up Leyden Street to the old church, then climbed the steps to Burial Hill. "Elder Brewster" held a service there.

"And we may be in it?" Nan asked.

Aunt Nan said the committee had invited the

Bobbseys to commemorate the first twins born in the old colony.

"Were they Bobbsey twins too?" Flossie asked.

Her aunt laughed and said no, their names were not Bobbsey. "But they were ancestors of ours." She arose from her Boston rocker and pulled a small book from a shelf under the window. Opening it, she read:

"Among the children of Edward Dotey and Sarah (Faunce) were Mary, born 9 July, 1671, at Plymouth; and Martha, born 9 July, 1671, at Plymouth."

"So Mary and Martha were twins," Mrs. Bobbsey remarked.

Aunt Nan said that they were the granddaughters of the original Edward Dotey of the "Mayflower."

Nan wrinkled her brow, puzzled. "But the twins weren't Pilgrims and weren't in the first parade," she said.

"That's right. For Friday's parade you children will play different parts. Nan, you'll be Mary Allerton, and Flossie will be her sister, whose name was Remember."

"What a funny name," Freddie said with a chuckle. "Who will I be, Aunt Nan?"

"Henry Sampson. He was a boy about your

age. And Bert will represent Richard More."

"Do we have to practice for the parade?" Freddie asked eagerly.

"It's not necessary, but you may want to," Aunt Nan replied.

"I want to be the drummer," the little boy said excitedly.

"May I carry a gun?" Bert asked. "Just like I've seen the men do in the Pilgrim pictures?"

As his aunt nodded, the doorbell rang. Before anyone could rise to answer it, a smiling boy and girl walked in. Aunt Nan introduced the tall, blond-haired boy of thirteen as Jack Hathaway. The brown-eyed girl, ten, was his sister Jane. They lived next door and had been waiting for the Bobbseys to come.

After the Hathaway children had shaken hands with Mrs. Bobbsey they started a lively chatter with the visiting twins.

"We'd like you to see our boat," Jack said. "It's at the yacht club."

"It's fun to sail in it," Jane added.

"May we go down there now?" Bert asked his mother.

"All right. But you and Nan take good care of Freddie and Flossie."

"We can swim," the small twins said in chorus.

"I know that." Mrs. Bobbsey smiled. "But watch out just the same."

With Jack Hathaway in the lead, the six children hurried off. On the way Bert asked if Jack and Jane knew a boy named George Rench.

The Hathaways exchanged glances. "Do you know him?" Jane asked.

"No, he's not a friend of ours," Nan said, and told how they had heard about George.

"We don't exactly like him," Jack remarked. "He's new around here and plays mean tricks."

"He has a sailboat, too," Jane said, "and he is always bumping into somebody."

"He and Danny will make a good team," said Bert. "We'd better watch our step!"

It did not take the children long to reach the yacht club. Jane pointed to a small sailboat bobbing on the water. "That's ours. We call it 'Leetle Beetle.' "

The Bobbseys laughed, then Bert said, "She's nifty!"

"Our 'Beetle's' ten feet long," Jack said. "Even though she has only one sail, she can really whiz."

"She's called a turnabout," his sister added. "You'll see when you're in her. First Jack and I will show you how she sails."

Jack asked Bert if he would row him and his

sister out to the "Leetle Beetle" and bring the
small boat back for other people to use. Upon
reaching the sailboat, the Hathaways climbed

in and unfurled the sail, which was half red and
half white.

"Oh, it's *bee-yoo-ti-ful!*" Flossie clapped her
hands as she watched the trim boat start across
the harbor.

After Jack and Jane had tacked back and
forth several times, they returned to the dock.

"Do you think I could sail her?" Bert asked Jack.

"Sure. Want to try it?"

As only two could get into the small boat it was decided that Bert would take Freddie for a ride. They stepped in. With Bert at the tiller and his brother in front of him, they started off.

A brisk southeast breeze swept across the harbor, and Bert skillfully sailed the boat back and forth. Now for the first time he noticed that Plymouth Harbor was protected by a long, sandy peninsula which stretched out into the bay several miles from the southern side of Plymouth.

After they had sailed back and forth for fifteen minutes, Bert said, "We'd better go back now, Freddie, and give the girls a turn."

As the brothers neared the yacht club, Freddie suddenly cried, "Look out, Bert!"

Heading toward them was another turnabout with a green sail. Her skipper seemed to be steering deliberately at "Leetle Beetle." Bert tried to swing the sail and rudder in an effort to get out of the way. But as he did, a sudden gust of wind billowed the sail. The boat tipped far over to one side.

Freddie had half risen to his feet. The boom shifted suddenly and swept the little boy overboard!

CHAPTER VII

A SECRET DRAWER

FREDDIE went down and down in the water. When he opened his eyes he could see nothing but murky water. The little boy fought to get back to the surface, but it seemed so far up.

Suddenly he spied a rope dangling almost in front of his face. Grabbing it, he pulled himself hand over hand to the top. By this time his lungs were nearly bursting for want of air.

"You okay?" cried Bert. "I was just coming after you." He hauled his brother into the sailboat.

At the same moment a motorboat pulled up alongside the brothers. At the wheel was a husky man of about thirty-five. He had a friendly face and wore what looked like a policeman's cap.

"I saw what happened and came over in case you were in trouble," the man said. Shielding his eyes from the sun, he glanced about the harbor. "There goes the sailboat that nearly rammed you."

"I wish we could chase her," said Bert.

"We'll do it," said the man. "Hop in here."

He assisted the boys into the motorboat, tied the Hathaways' craft onto the stern, and set off after the boat with the green sail. Two boys were in it. Coming alongside, Bert was amazed to see Danny Rugg and George Rench.

The motorboat was throttled down, and its pilot called out:

"You fellows will have to obey the rules of the harbor, or you won't be allowed to sail!"

"All right," George replied grudgingly.

As Danny and his friend sailed off, the man with the blue cap said, "I've had trouble with that Rench boy before." Then he smiled at the Bobbseys. "My name is Mack Donald," he said. "I'm the harbor master."

Hearing this, Freddie's eyes grew wide. "Do you have charge of this whole harbor?"

The man smiled and nodded. "I'm sort of a water policeman," he said.

"Thanks for helping us, Mr. Donald," Bert remarked gratefully. "I'm Bert Bobbsey, and this is my brother Freddie."

"Just call me Mack. Everyone else does," the man said.

He asked if the boys wanted to transfer to

their own boat or go to the yacht club dock with him.

"I've had enough sailing," said Freddie. "I'll stay with you."

On the way in Mack said, "A Pilgrim on the 'Mayflower' saved himself in just the same way you did, Freddie."

"Tell me about it," the little boy requested.

The harbor master said that John Howland was swept off the "Mayflower" by a large wave. When he was about fifteen feet under water he grabbed a topsail rope and saved himself.

"Jiminy!" Freddie exclaimed. "You mean I acted just like a Pilgrim?"

"You certainly did," Mack replied, smiling, and pulled up at the dock, where the other children were waiting.

Jack took the mooring rope of "Leetle Beetle" which Mack held toward him. Freddie was sorry to have to leave the harbor master.

"Before you go, please tell us about the ghost of Clark's Island," he said.

"So you've heard about the ghost too." Mack grinned. "Maybe there is one, maybe there isn't. Some folks think it's purely imaginary—the strange lights and the queer doings on the island."

Jane spoke up. "Mother thinks maybe it's just someone playing ghost walk," she said.

When the Bobbseys looked blank, Jane quickly explained the game. It was something like hide-and-seek. While the children were "it," their parents would put sheets about themselves and hide in the woods.

"When the children go to find them, the grownups pretend to scare them by jumping from this hiding place and that."

"I'd like to play that game," said Nan.

"Ghost or no ghost," said Mack as he prepared to shove off, "there's one slippery spector I'd like to lay my hands on."

"What do you mean?" Bert asked.

Mack said that a thief had been active in Plymouth for several weeks. "He's been stealing small antiques of great value from the exhibits."

"Have you ever seen him?" Bert asked.

"No," the harbor master replied, "but two people have reported seeing the thief escape in a motorboat. I'm on the lookout for him."

Nan thought immediately of the suspicious stranger who had tried to sell her mother some antiques on the train. She told Mr. Donald about him.

"You say he had a pewter pitcher in his bag?" Mack asked, extremely interested. "A pitcher was among the things stolen. Thanks very much for the clue. I'll pass the information on to the Plymouth police."

Mack now waved good-by and started back to the town dock where he kept his boat. By this time the hot August sun had completely dried Freddie's clothes.

"I like the harbor master," he said as Nan set out to give Flossie a sail in the "Leetle Beetle."

As the boys waited, Bert said, "Jack, do you suppose we could go out to Clark's Island tomorrow?"

"And look for the ghost?"

"Yes."

Jack said that currents at the harbor mouth were too tricky for him to risk taking the sailboat, and he had no motorboat.

Jane spoke up. "Let's ask Mack. Maybe he'll take us."

"That's a good idea!" her brother said.

After Nan and Flossie returned and Bert and Jack had moored the "Leetle Beetle," the children hurried to the town dock. They found the harbor master in his office.

"Well, what can I do for you?"

"Take us to the ghost," Freddie chirped.

Mr. Donald tilted back in his old captain's chair, lifted his cap, and scratched his head. "I'll tell you what," he said. "I'll be free tomorrow at one-thirty. Suppose I take you over then in my small boat."

After a pause he said that unfortunately he

could not take all the children. "So perhaps Nan and Bert and the Hathaways can go this time." He smiled at Freddie and Flossie. "You can go to Clark's Island some other time."

On the way home Jane told the Bobbseys about friends of theirs who lived on the island. "Their name is Woodson. Mary Jo is my age. Her daddy's not living; just her mother and grandmother."

Jack said that because there were only a few children on the island, Mary Jo loved to have the Hathaways visit them. "We'll have fun and maybe play ghost walk."

When the Bobbseys reached Aunt Nan's they eagerly told her and their mother about the proposed trip. Aunt Nan chuckled. "I knew you twins would soon be on the trail of the ghost. And I'll bet you catch him before you leave Plymouth!"

Mrs. Bobbsey smiled. "I rather think myself they might."

Next morning, after they finished breakfast, Aunt Nan said, "I'd like to show you some of the real old places in town, including the salt box house."

"You mean there was just salt in it?" Flossie inquired.

Aunt Nan smiled. "I don't wonder you asked that. It means the roof of the square house was just like the top of an old-fashioned salt box. The Howlands built it nearly three hundred years ago."

When the twins saw it, they were intrigued by the roof which slanted down close to the ground in the rear.

The Bobbseys next made their way to Pilgrim Hall. It had been built in 1824 to honor the first settlers.

"Look at all the things in here!" Freddie exclaimed, dashing from one exhibit to another.

Flossie liked the crib that Peregrine White, the first child born in the colony, had slept in. "I wish I had it for my dollies," she whispered to her sister.

Besides old chairs and tables there was a model of the "Mayflower," and also the hull of a boat named the "Sparrowhawk."

"I'm sorry to tell you," said Aunt Nan, "that the 'Sparrowhawk' was wrecked not far from here. It wasn't so lucky as the 'Mayflower.'"

Freddie had wandered off to look at an exhibit of weapons and armor used at the time of the Pilgrims. On display were the swords of Governor Carver, Elder Brewster, and Miles Standish.

"I wish I could play with one of them," the little boy thought wistfully.

Freddie ran to ask permission to do this,

but Aunt Nan said she wanted to show them the Mayflower Society House.

She led them past her own home on North Street. Near the end of the block they crossed over and entered a walk flanked by two giant old linden trees. The house before them was spacious from its cupola on top to its wide rambling porches.

Leading the way, Aunt Nan rang a bell on the right side of the doorway. Presently a man with a friendly smile appeared. He was short and had black hair flecked with gray.

"Good morning," he said, holding the door open for his visitors. "I'm glad you came," he told Aunt Nan. "Are your friends also members of the Society?"

She explained that they were descendants of Edward Dotey like herself. The man introduced himself as Mr. Rogers, custodian for the day, and said Edward Dotey was his ancestor too.

"He was naughty, wasn't he?" Flossie asked, remembering how Edward Dotey had tried to jump onto Clark's Island ahead of the first mate.

"Impatient," Mr. Rogers said with a sheepish grin. "But I think his descendants have more than made up for his peccadillos."

Flossie said her mother made peccadillos from green tomatoes and it smelled nice while it was cooking.

This made Mr. Rogers laugh, and he said, "Don't you mean piccalilli? I believe a peccadillo is a slight offense."

The Bobbsey family signed the guest register in the large center hall. Then Mr. Rogers said he would take them on a tour of the house. "It was built by the great-grandson of the Pilgrims' Governor Winslow."

Stepping from the hall into the living room, Freddie glanced up at the unusually high doorway. "Did the Indian Massasoit ever live here," the boy asked, "on account of he was so tall?"

Mr. Rogers laughed and explained that Massasoit was not so tall as his statue indicated. "He probably lived in a wigwam."

Next the man pointed out the living-room fireplace decorated with religious scenes on delft tiles from Holland.

"Oh, there's Jonah swallowing the whale— I mean the whale swallowing Jonah!" said Nan.

Giggling, the children followed Mr. Rogers up the stairs to the third-floor cupola. While the others were looking out the windows, Flossie saw a small-sized high silk hat on a table. She tugged at Mr. Rogers' sleeve. "May I try it on?" she asked. "And whose is it?"

"I don't know where it came from. It must have belonged to either a tiny man or a large boy."

Flossie put the hat on her head. It fitted, and Nan said her sister looked cute in it—like Tom Thumb. "Maybe the hat was made for the Governor's son," she suggested.

Mr. Rogers said the mysterious old hat had been made long after this time. The Bobbseys thanked him for showing them the interesting home, then said good-by.

The next stop on their tour was another historical house, which was in charge of Mr. John Warren. After he had shown the visitors around, the children went back to look at various exhibits which intrigued them. Freddie hurried off to see the old swords and armor.

The little boy gazed admiringly at the model of a soldier encased in armor. He reached up to feel the thickness of the breastplate.

"I wonder if this comes off," Freddie said to himself. Secretly he had an idea that he might try on the armor. As he tugged at it, the soldier began to teeter back and forth.

"Look out!" Nan cried out from across the room.

Mrs. Bobbsey, hearing her, turned around. The soldier was about to crash! The custodian in charge saw it at the same time, and the two raced forward. They pushed the soldier back just in time.

"Oh, I'm sorry," said Freddie quickly.

The soldier was about to crash!

Mr. Warren said it was all right. "But if you want to play Miles Standish, young fellow, I think you'd better make a suit of armor out of cardboard."

He now explained a little more about a small flat-top desk. Nan was particularly interested in the old piece.

"This is believed to have come over on another seventeenth century ship," Mr. Warren said.

"Then it's as old as a Pilgrim," stated Flossie, examining the curious carving on top of the desk.

"What do you see on it?" Aunt Nan asked the twins.

They examined the markings carefully, then Freddie said, "It looks like a woman hanging clothes on a line."

Mr. Warren laughed. "Well, not exactly," he said. "What do you see, Nan?"

"A dove."

"Good for you!" he said. "That's what it is. Whoever carved the desk probably made the dove as a symbol of the peace which they hoped to find in the new world."

The Bobbseys were curious about the old desk. Nan dropped down to her hands and knees and looked beneath it. Suddenly she exclaimed:

"Look! I think it has a secret panel."

"Where?" Mr. Warren asked in amazement.

"Up underneath here," Nan said as she crawled beneath the ancient piece of furniture.

With Bert's help Mr. Warren carefully turned the desk on its side. Sure enough, there were faint lines which indicated that the old piece might have a hidden compartment.

"Let's open it!" Nan said excitedly.

CHAPTER VIII

A SPLASHY RIDE

THE twins begged to open the secret compartment in the ancient desk immediately.

"I'll get a hammer," Freddie offered, glancing about.

Mr. Warren chuckled. "Not so fast," he said. "We'll have to get permission before we do this kind of sleuthing."

The man explained that the family which had given the desk to the Warren exhibit would have to be notified first. "Once we get their okay," Mr. Warren said, smiling, "we can pry open the secret panel."

Seeing the disappointed look on the faces of the four children, Mr. Warren added quickly, "I didn't know you were such good detectives. I have another little mystery you might solve."

"Oh boy!" Bert said, rubbing his hands together. "We'll do our best, Mr. Warren. What is it?"

The man excused himself and left the room for a moment. When he returned, he was holding a curious object in his hands. "Do you know what this is?" he asked.

"The hilt of a sword," Bert answered.

"And a very old one, too," Mr. Warren explained.

He said the hilt had been dug up from the yard of the house. It had been examined many times by experts, but nobody could determine its origin.

"There are three possibilities," Mr. Warren said. "First, it may have been left by one of the early Pilgrims. But I doubt that myself."

"Then who do you think owned it?" Bert asked.

"I think it was left here," Mr. Warren continued, "either by the French explorer Champlain or by Captain John Smith."

"I didn't know either of those men was ever in Plymouth," Mrs. Bobbsey said with a look of surprise.

Mr. Warren told them that Champlain had been in that area in 1605, before the Pilgrims landed. And Captain John Smith had visited the place in 1614.

"I suppose the missing blade would solve the mystery," Bert stated.

Mr. Warren said it should. "I think some inscription must have been carved on the blade to identify its owner."

Instantly Freddie wished to dig in the lovely gardens behind the house to find it.

"That's been done already," Mr. Warren told him and added, "This will probably remain as one of those unsolved mysteries of history."

At this Aunt Nan spoke up. "Don't be too sure of that, Mr. Warren. My nieces and nephews have solved several mysteries."

"I hope they can solve this one," the man said. Then his face took on a sad look. "But I'd rather have them find the old pewter pitcher."

"What pitcher was that?" Nan asked.

Mr. Warren told the visitors that the thief who had been plaguing the exhibits about Plymouth had stolen a valuable pewter pitcher.

"Mother!" Nan exclaimed. "Maybe that *was* the same pitcher I saw in the man's black bag on the train!"

Mrs. Bobbsey said this was indeed possible. Nan told Mr. Warren the story and said they had given the clue to the harbor master.

"That's fine," Mr. Warren said as he escorted the group to the front door. "Drop around again before you leave and let me know how you're making out with your detective work."

After luncheon at Aunt Nan's, the older twins met Jack and Jane Hathaway. They hurried off to the town dock. Mack, who was waiting, led them down a wooden ramp to his motorboat.

Nan, Jane, and Jack climbed into the front seat, while Bert sat behind them alongside Mr. Donald. The harbor master gunned the motor and started slowly toward the first channel

marker. Increasing speed, the boat zipped along, churning up a foamy white wake.

"How long is your boat?" Bert asked, leaning toward Mack so that he could be heard above the roar of the engine.

"Thirteen footer with a twenty-five horse-power outboard motor."

"She goes like the wind!"

Farther out in the harbor the boat zoomed through choppy little waves, sending up a misty spray on the occupants.

"Whee! I'm getting wet!" Nan said. Turning around, she caught Mack's eye and pointed to the polished deck of the hull.

The harbor master smiled and nodded. Nan climbed out on the bow and sat with her legs straddling the front of the motorboat. The wind rumpled her hair as she turned her head to wave back at the others.

Mack carefully followed the channel markers, skirting around shoals which showed above water at low tide.

"Any clamming over there?" Bert shouted.

Mack shook his head. "Nothing but mussels," he replied. "The clams disappeared from here quite a while ago."

Soon they neared the protecting peninsula of Plymouth beach. Mack turned the boat sharply to the left, running parallel to the sandy shore toward the promontory at the end.

Not far from the tip of the promontory stood a small lighthouse. "That's called the Bug Light," Jack called out.

Nan smiled and turned to Jane. "Is that why you call your boat 'Leetle Beetle'?" she teased.

The squat-looking lighthouse rose straight out of the water like an Indian arrowhead. Mack told Bert it was occupied by coast guardsmen. As they passed the light two men stepped out on the railing high above them and waved down at the passing motorboat.

"Look! I see two islands over there," Bert said.

"The one to the left is Clark's Island," Mack remarked. Then he added, "The land to the right is not an island at all. That's Saquish Head, the end of a peninsula which curves around to the mainland at Duxbury."

Bert guessed that Saquish must be an Indian name.

"It is," Mack said, grinning. "It means 'many clams.' Too bad most of them disappeared."

He steered directly toward Clark's Island. By this time the tide had receded even farther so the boat came into shallow water some distance from the shoreline.

Mack cut the motor. "Okay, children," he said. "All out!"

They thanked him for the ride. Then holding their shoes in their hands, they got out of the boat and started to wade ashore.

"I'll come back for you later," the harbor master told them and backed into deeper water.

There were only a few houses on the island. From one shore-front cottage dashed a girl wearing shorts and a white jersey.

"Here comes Mary Jo Woodson," said Jane.
"Come on, kids, let's meet her."

In a few minutes the five came together on the
sandy shore. Mary Jo was a plump, dark-haired
girl with dimples. She said she was happy that
Jack and Jane had come to play with her and
was glad they had brought the Bobbseys.

"This must be a great place to spend the summer," Bert remarked as the visitors put on their
shoes.

"It's a little lonesome, but we don't mind that
usually," the girl replied, leading the way to the
Woodson cottage. "It's been kind of spooky this
summer, though."

"You mean the ghost?" Bert asked.

"Well, I don't really think it's a ghost," Mary
Jo said, dimpling. "We think there's an intruder
on our island. We don't know who he is. Police
searched the island once but couldn't find anyone."

"We'd like to help you hunt for him," Bert
spoke up.

"He's always around after dark," Mary Jo
said. "Well, what would you like to do now?"

Jack spoke up. "I thought Nan and Bert
might like to see Pulpit Rock."

"Sure. We can go there right away. Come on!"

Mary Jo led the children along a path through
the scrubby growth which covered Clark's Is-

land. Before reaching the rock, they came to a large well at the side of the path beneath a towering tree.

"We carry all our drinking water from here," Mary Jo explained as she lowered a bucket on the end of a long chain. "Want a drink?"

"Oh, yes," everyone answered.

When the bucket had filled with water from deep in the well, Bert pulled it up. The water was cool and delicious.

As Jack was taking a drink the children were suddenly startled by a strange laughing sound. It seemed to come from among the bushes.

"What's that?" Nan asked.

"I never heard it before," Mary Jo whispered.

The high-pitched laugh came again. It was eerie. They all wondered if it could be the ghost.

"I'm going to find out who that is," Jack said with determination.

The two boys stepped into the thick brush and peered about. All at once Bert heard a crashing sound in the underbrush.

CHAPTER IX

PULPIT ROCK

AS THE children stood watchful and a little frightened, a large, black dog bounded from the undergrowth toward Bert.

Suddenly Mary Jo called out, "Tui! Stop that!"

Instantly the dog ceased his headlong dash. He ran to Mary Jo, wagging his tail.

Bert felt very relieved. "Is he your dog?"

"Yes."

"Well one thing is sure," said Bert. "Tui didn't laugh. I still think it was the ghost. Let's get Tui to help us find him."

They searched for several minutes, but neither the children nor the dog could find anyone.

"It's spooky all right," said Nan, as they gave up and started once more for Pulpit Rock. "Mary Jo, where did your dog get his name?"

As Mary Jo bent down to pat Tui, she said,

"I read in a book once that in the Fiji Islands it's the name for king. So instead of calling my dog King, I decided on Tui."

"It's a pretty name," said Nan.

In another minute Mary Jo said, "We're nearly to Pulpit Rock."

They continued along the path. Finally the children came to a large clearing. At the end of it lay a huge rock.

"It's as big as a house!" Bert exclaimed in amazement, and hurried over to examine it.

"How do you suppose it got here on the island?" Nan wanted to know.

Mary Jo said that geologists thought the rock had been pushed there by a glacier when the world was a lot younger.

"The Pilgrims must have been impressed by it," Bert said.

Approaching the base of the rock, Bert scrambled up to the top of the sloping stone. Mary Jo, meanwhile, led Nan around to the left side of the boulder.

"Here is where the Pilgrims prayed," she said and pointed to an inscription carved in the rock. It read:

ON THE SABBOTH DAY
WEE RESTED

"Governor Bradford wrote those words in his

diary," Jane said, "and they were later carved in the rock."

"I wonder how the Pilgrims felt when they landed here?" Nan mused aloud.

Mary Jo said the small boat in which these men were exploring the coast on Friday, December 18, 1620, was hit by a bad storm. Its mast and rudder broken, the boat was driven to the island. The crew mended it on Saturday, but on Sunday, they only rested and prayed and would not set out for the mainland in their shallop until the next day.

Nan asked what a shallop was, and Jack explained that it was a small, open sailboat.

"But not as tiny as our turnabout," Jane remarked with a twinkle in her eyes.

While the children sat on the rock and chatted, Tui was busy nosing about the base of the great stone.

"Maybe Tui has discovered a clue to the ghost," Nan said. "Let's follow him."

She led the others as they scrambled off the rock and followed Tui through the dense brush. But after fifteen minutes of fruitless search, Jack said, "Tui was probably only on the trail of a rabbit."

Bert and Nan disagreed. They were sure the dog had picked up the trail of the person with the strange laugh.

"We're near the cemetery, aren't we?" Jack said as they trudged along.

"What cemetery?" Nan asked.

Mary Jo said her family's old burial ground was close by. "Would you like to see the place? It dates back to about 1850."

"Yes," said the Bobbseys and thought, "That's the trail Tui took."

Mary Jo found the nearly overgrown path, which led deeper into the woods. "There's the cemetery," she said, pointing to a clearing.

It was a gloomy spot, well shaded by surrounding trees. The perimeter of the small cemetery was marked by the gray trunks of dead cedar trees. A little shiver ran up and down Nan's spine as she gazed at their gnarled and twisted branches.

A few old weathered tombstones lay at crooked angles, while others had fallen to the ground. Mary Jo explained that many years before, her ancestors had farmed the island. "Most of them are buried here," she said.

"I wonder how they'd like it if they knew we play 'ghost walk' here," Jane remarked.

"They wouldn't mind, I'm sure," said Mary Jo. "Sometime we must play it with the Bobbseys."

Nan said she had heard of the game and added

that it must be very scary, especially on a dark night.

"You'll see," Jane told her, giving Mary Jo a knowing wink.

Bert and Nan became interested in reading the old dates and strange epitaphs on the tombstones. No one noticed the disappearance of Tui. Suddenly they heard the strange laughter again, then the distant bark of Tui.

"I hope he's caught the ghost," Bert said. "Come on, let's find out!"

As the children started into the underbrush, the laughter grew louder and jolly. A moment later Tui sprang into view. Behind him ran two children, giggling.

"So!" Mary Jo said, standing with her hands on her hips and making a wry face. "You're the sillies who were laughing. I'm glad Tui caught you!"

She introduced the children as Helen and Lance Goodwin, who also spent summers on the island. Helen, a red-haired girl with freckles, was eleven. Lance, a handsome, fair-haired boy, was twelve. The Goodwins said they had seen the visitors through their field glasses and had decided to have a little fun by scaring everybody.

"Did you see anything of the ghost," Jack

asked, "while you were prowling around the woods?"

Helen said she had seen a figure flit among the trees but decided that perhaps it was only a shadow. Upon hearing that the Bobbseys were trying to find the ghost of Clark's Island, she and Lance wished the twins luck.

"If you need our help, just call on us," Lance said. Then he snapped his fingers. "Say, we have enough kids to play 'Capture the Flag.' "

"What's that?" Bert asked.

Mary Jo explained that it was a game the local children liked to play. Because there were so few boys and girls on Clark's Island they seldom had the opportunity.

"Come on," Jack said. "There's an open field near Mary Jo's house. We can play there."

When they reached the field, Mary Jo ran into the house and returned with two pieces of white cloth. Jack tied each of them to a stick which he pushed into the ground on either side of the field. Then he made a white chalk line down the center of the grass.

"We need one more player to have four on each side," he said.

"I'll get Russell Cook," Lance offered and dashed off to a cottage half hidden in the woods about a quarter of a mile away.

Russell was a short, stocky boy of ten with

stubby blond hair and a wide grin. After he had been introduced to the newcomers, Lance said, "Bert, you and I will pick sides. You choose first."

Bert quickly called his sister, Jack, and Jane. That left Lance with Mary Jo, Helen, and Russell.

Mary Jo explained that each team lined up on opposite sides of the chalk mark. "Then we try to pull each other over," she said. "Once you've been pulled into 'enemy' territory, you're captured."

"Yes, but don't let anyone on the opposite side dash over to capture the flag," Jack warned. "That's the idea of the game."

"Everybody understand it?" Jane asked.

When the Bobbseys nodded, Mary Jo said, "Let's go!"

Standing firmly on either side of the line the children made lightning-like motions to grab their opponents. Russell grasped Nan's wrist and was just about to pull her over the line when Bert came to his sister's aid. Putting his arms around her waist, he pulled her back and Russell came with her!

"You're my prisoner!" Nan cried.

Now it was three to four. But not for long. Helen quickly grabbed Jack by the shirt. Even though the boy had the advantage in weight, he stumbled, falling across the line into enemy territory.

The fight was even again at three to three. The tussle went on. Bert Bobbsey moved away from the opposing groups. Suddenly he made a dash for the flag. Seeing this, Mary Jo cried out:

"Stop him! Stop him!"

With the speed of a deer, Bert grabbed the enemy flag and raced toward home territory. Lance leaped toward his opponent but missed Bert's arm by inches. Bert Bobbsey scampered over the line.

"We win! We win!" Jack called out.

"Boy, you Bobbseys sure are fast players!" Lance said as he congratulated the winners.

As they started to leave, Nan said, "Say, where did the other flag go?"

Everybody turned to look. The fluttering white cloth had disappeared!

"The ghost again!" said Jane.

But just then Tui came around the house, the flagpole between his teeth.

"Maybe Tui is the ghost of Clark's Island," Bert said jokingly.

Since it was nearly time for the visitors to meet the harbor master, Mary Jo escorted them inside her bungalow to meet her mother and grandmother. The younger Mrs. Woodson was

Bert Bobbsey scampered over the line

a stout, jolly woman, suntanned from her stay on the island.

The grandmother had dimples like Mary Jo, and her blond hair had only a few wisps of gray in it. When she heard that the Bobbseys had come to find the ghost, she put her knitting into her lap. Leaning forward in her chair, she asked, "Would you like a real good clue?"

"Yes, Mrs. Woodson. Have you found one?" Nan asked eagerly.

"I have a theory," the elderly woman said. "There's a boat that comes over from Saquish Head. The fellow steering it always bends low, so his face is hidden. I've watched him through my binoculars. I feel sure he's the ghost."

The children were startled by this, and Nan was about to ask her a question when they heard someone calling from the beach. Mary Jo ran to the door. "It's Mr. Donald calling for you."

The Woodsons invited the children to come again soon. Mary Jo's mother escorted them to the beach.

"It certainly has clouded up a lot," she remarked. "You children had better hurry before you get into a fog."

The tide was coming in now, and the motorboat was nearer the beach. When they had taken their seats, Mack started the motor, but he had a worried look in his eyes.

"Is something wrong with the outboard?" Bert asked him, but the motor sputtered to life.

"No," the harbor master replied. "I'm worried about the weather. There's a heavy fog rolling in."

At first Mack headed toward Saquish Head, following a channel he knew well. Then he turned to the right in the direction of the Bug Light. On their way a haze filled the air and grew thicker and thicker. Mack looked more worried than ever.

"I'm afraid the fog is going to overtake us," he said.

Soon a dense blanket of mist billowed about them.

"I should have brought my compass!" the harbor master said as they all peered into the pea-soup fog.

Mack throttled back the motor, then said, "We're completely lost!"

CHAPTER X

FUN AT THE BUG LIGHT

ALTHOUGH they were lost in the fog, Bert and Nan remained calm. So did Jack and Jane.

Mack was chagrined. "This hasn't happened to me since I was a boy," he said and told of another time when he had been fogbound on a small boat.

"What'll we do now?" Nan asked him.

"Our only hope is to find the Bug Light," the harbor master replied.

"Will it help to drive around slowly in circles?" Bert asked. He remembered doing this once on the lake at home in a fog.

"It's a good plan," said Mack.

With the motor turning the propeller slowly, he set the rudder so that the boat would go round and round in ever widening circles.

After twenty minutes of searching, Jane said, "I see a pink light, Mack."

"Where?"

"Over there," she said, pointing.

"It must be the Bug Light!" Mack said and steered the craft toward the glow, which grew brighter as they approached it.

The skipper did not see the lighthouse until he nearly bumped into it. Drifting alongside the gray steel structure, Mack called up to the coastguardmen. A minute later his call was answered.

"We got lost!" Mack told the man.

"Better stay here then. Climb the ladder!" the coastguardman answered.

The motorboat putt-putted around the Bug Light until they found the ladder which rose directly out of the water. Bert grasped the metal rungs, and Jack tied the craft to one of them. Then the children climbed up the ladder, followed by Mack, and soon were standing on the platform which circled the lighthouse.

Two strapping young coastguardmen, both over six feet tall, greeted the unexpected callers. The men wore khaki trousers and blue denim shirts. Their sleeves were rolled high on their arms, showing tattoos of sailing ships and anchors.

"Hi, Pete! Hi, Ralph!" said Mack.

The coastguardmen grinned. "We didn't expect the harbor master to get lost!" Ralph teased.

"Quit your ribbing," Mack said good-naturedly. "Accidents will happen. Besides, why did your weather bureau order this fog?" he teased them.

He introduced the children, then Bert asked, "How long do you think the fog will last?"

Pete said the forecast was not good. "We expect it to hang here until tomorrow morning," he said.

Nan looked worried. What would her mother and aunt think if the children did not return that night?

Ralph seemed to sense Nan's alarm. "There's nothing to worry about, miss," he said kindly. "We'll radio ashore and have your folks told that you're okay."

He led the children inside the tower of the lighthouse, which contained one large room. In it were the men's sleeping quarters, a galley, radio, and other equipment.

"Make yourselves at home," Ralph said, motioning to comfortable-looking chairs. "I'll get this message off right away."

Seating himself at the radio table, the guardman phoned his message by short wave to the coast station. He arranged that the Plymouth police would be notified. They, in turn, would tell Mrs. Bobbsey, the Hathaways, and Mr. Donald's family where the wanderers were.

"How about some chow?" Ralph asked. "You folks must be hungry."

"Sounds good," said Jack.

Pete winked at his partner. "Shall we break out the steaks, skipper?" he suggested. "These are special guests, you know."

Bert grinned. "In story books the poor coast-guardmen have only pork and beans to eat."

"Not nowadays," said Pete. He told them that they had a freeze locker operated by an electric generator. "Nothing but the best for us!"

"He's recruiting for the Coast Guard," Ralph remarked with a wink at Bert and Jack. "How would you like to sign up?"

Nan and Jane giggled. "Maybe we could be lady coastguardmen," Nan said with a chuckle as Pete began to prepare the meal.

While they were waiting, Bert asked the coast-guardmen if they had seen any strange boats in the area recently.

"Come to think of it," Ralph remarked, "there has been a strange fellow who puts in at Saquish Head. He keeps unusual hours."

Bert and Nan were interested at once and asked what the hours were.

"It's either early in the morning or late in the evening. It almost seems as if he doesn't want to be seen."

"He might be the ghost of Clark's Island," Jack ventured.

"Or the thief I'm looking for," Mack said as the group began to eat steak sandwiches.

The coastguardmen, thinking they might have uncovered a clue, promised to keep an eye on the fellow with their powerful telescope.

Bert suddenly had an idea. "Is there anything on Saquish Head that man might be interested in?"

Ralph replied that at the exact spot where the man landed his boat there was nothing but the remains of old Fort Standish.

"Where is it?" Nan asked. "I didn't see any fort as we passed near there."

Mack Donald explained that the fort, built during the Revolution to protect Plymouth Harbor, had long since crumbled into ruins.

"I understand the only things left are some hidden passageways," he said. "But they're underground, so you can't see them."

Ralph volunteered the information that a certain historical society planned to dig in the ruins soon in an effort to uncover some interesting historical relics.

"Maybe that's what the stranger in the motorboat is doing," Jane suggested.

"Could be," Mack agreed.

At the end of the meal a radio message came

to the Bug Light. Ralph jotted it down, then turned to the others. "Here's some news from the Plymouth police," he said.

As the children listened eagerly, Ralph told them a valuable pair of candlesticks had been stolen from Mr. Warren's historical house a few hours before. The thief had made his escape in a boat, apparently knowing that the harbor master was off duty.

"And here's some more interesting information," Ralph went on. "It's about two boys named Danny Rugg and George Rench."

"We know Danny well," said Bert. "What's happened to them?"

Ralph reported that the two boys had been reported missing after a day of sightseeing by themselves. "The police haven't found them yet, and have sent out an alarm by radio."

"Oh dear," said Nan. "I hope they're not in trouble."

"That's right," Bert agreed. "Maybe we can join in the search when we get home tomorrow."

As bunks were assigned to the stranded party, Bert and Nan continued to wonder about Danny and George. But finally the twins fell asleep.

Mack aroused everyone at daybreak. The fog had lifted. After a hearty breakfast of bacon and eggs they thanked Ralph and Pete, then climbed down the ladder to their boat.

Mack held the motor at top speed, and some time later the voyagers were gliding alongside the town dock. Mrs. Bobbsey, Freddie, and Flossie were there to meet them, along with Mrs. Hathaway.

"I wish I could have slept at the Bug Light," Freddie said wistfully.

"But wasn't it scary in the fog?" Flossie asked.

"It was fun," Nan replied.

Mrs. Hathaway left with her children, and the Bobbseys walked toward North Street.

"Flossie and I found a firehouse!" Freddie told the older twins excitedly as they climbed the steps on Cole's Hill. "They have special trucks for forest fires, and a rescue boat on a trailer, too."

"Sounds interesting," said Bert. "I'll have to see them."

Flossie said she and Freddie had learned a lot about Plymouth. "It's a hundred and six square miles."

"With twenty-six miles of coast line," Freddie added importantly.

"And 365 ponds," Flossie chattered on. "One for every day in the year."

Mrs. Bobbsey laughed. "They learned all this from Fire Chief Holt," she said. "But I was surprised to hear that Plymouth is the largest town in area in Massachusetts."

Bert and Nan told what they had heard about the theft from the Warren house and said they would like to stop in to ask more about it. When they did, Mr. Warren sadly told the story of a man who had come in disguised as a very old fellow.

"He took the candlesticks and disappeared out the back door," Mr. Warren said. "While he was running away a false mustache fell off."

"Was he the man with the scar?" Nan asked anxiously.

"I'm afraid he was," Mr. Warren said. "I followed him, but he got away in a motorboat."

The Bobbseys promised to do all they could to help him recover the candlesticks, as well as the old pewter pitcher. The family said good-by and went on to Aunt Nan Shaw's house.

At once Nan phoned to police headquarters and asked if Danny and George had been found. When told no, she said the Bobbseys would like to help in the search.

"Glad to have you," the chief said.

When Nan told the others, Bert said, "Maybe Danny and George are hiding somewhere in town just to act smart. Why don't we look in all the historical buildings?"

This was agreed upon, and the four twins set out. Within an hour they had covered all the places they had already seen, peering into cupboards and closets. The missing boys were not in any of them.

Presently they came to First House with its wide boards and thatched roof. The children got permission to climb into the loft, thinking

Danny and George might be hiding there. They were disappointed.

As they came down again, Flossie said, "I feel more and more like a Pilgrim!"

The woman in charge laughed and said, "Wait until you see the fort."

The old fort was a replica of the one built by the original settlers. Inside on the first floor was a large meeting room, and upstairs on a deck were mounted cannon for the defense of the town.

"Oh, they aren't real ones," Freddie said, disappointed. "They're only wooden!"

"That's so eager beavers like you won't set them off," Bert said with a wink at Nan.

It was growing dark by the time the children finished their search of the town.

They walked to the top of Cole's Hill and looked out over the harbor. All at once Bert grabbed his twin's arm. He pointed toward Clark's Island. "Look over there!"

A red glare rose from the center of the island. "I'll bet that's Danny and he's setting off one of the flares he took from the train!" Bert declared.

"Let's tell Mack right away," Nan urged.

The four children hurried over to the town dock and told the harbor master their suspicions.

He shook his head. "That light couldn't have been made by Danny," he said.

"Are you sure?" Nan asked.

"I've just heard from the local police," Mack said, "that Danny and George were seen fourteen miles south of here this afternoon."

"Where?" Bert asked.

"At the Edaville railroad," Mack replied.

CHAPTER XI

A TINY TOWN

DANNY and George had gone off on a train! The Bobbseys were amazed.

"Will you tell me about the railroad?" Bert asked the harbor master.

Mack told them that the railroad was a tourist attraction in the cranberry bogs. It was a small railroad, but not a miniature. "It carries passengers. But the rails are only two feet apart and the train was really built to carry crates of cranberries from the bogs to the loading platforms."

"Danny and George must have gone there to have some fun," Nan remarked. She felt rather relieved.

"Or get into mischief," was Bert's guess.

When Mack told them the railroad was well worth seeing, Freddie said, "Let's go!"

In a few minutes the children were back at Aunt Nan's. When Mrs. Bobbsey heard their story, she agreed to take them on the train trip.

"And I hope we find Danny and George," said Nan. "It's mean of them to worry Mr. and Mrs. Rench."

When Mrs. Bobbsey asked directions to the railroad, Aunt Nan told her it was situated at South Carver. Bert inquired how they could get there.

"Too bad there's no public transportation," Aunt Nan said. "Maybe you could rent a car."

"Perhaps the Hathaways would take us," Nan spoke up.

"I think they would be glad to," Miss Shaw said. "Jack and Jane have been there many times and could show you around."

Bert and Nan hurried next door. They returned in a few minutes, smiling. Mrs. Hathaway had offered the Bobbseys her station wagon. Jack and Jane would go along and direct them to South Carver.

"We'll go early in the morning," Nan said.

"Hurrah!" cried Freddie. He turned a somersault, then made a shrieking sound like a locomotive.

"Oh, Freddie!" his mother exclaimed, covering her ears.

Shortly after breakfast the next day the Bobbseys heard a car horn in front of Aunt Nan's house. Hurrying out, they saw Mrs. Hathaway stepping out of her station wagon.

"Have a good time," she said, smiling. "I'm sorry I can't go with you."

"We are, too. And thank you very much," said Mrs. Bobbsey.

She got behind the wheel. As soon as the six children were in the car, the twins' mother started off along a road to the south of Plymouth. After riding through rolling country sprinkled with small pine trees, they came to a fork in the road.

"Turn right here, Mrs. Bobbsey," Jack directed.

"Are we getting close to the cranberry railroad?" Freddie asked eagerly.

"There it is right ahead," Jane spoke up.

"Wow, it has a regular railroad station!" the little boy exclaimed as his mother drove into a large parking lot near it.

The long, low building bore a sign reading: *Cranberry Junction.* On the other side of the tracks stretched thousands of acres of cranberries growing in soft, wet ground. In the center of the bogs and built above them was a large fresh-water reservoir.

"Cranberries need lots of water," Jack said when asked about the reservoir. "The farmers fill the bogs during a dry spell, and in the early spring whenever a frost or icy winds threaten to kill the blossoms, the bogs are flooded to protect the cranberry plants from them."

The Bobbseys and their friends hurried into the station where Mrs. Bobbsey bought tickets for the train ride. Just then the wailing sound of a locomotive whistle drifted across the bogs.

"It's coming! It's coming!" Freddie shouted, dashing out to the platform.

A distant plume of black smoke showed that the Edaville locomotive was headed toward the station for its first run of the day.

"Oh boy!" cried Freddie as the puffing engine pulled into the station amid the shouts of the children. He stood in awe while the escaping steam made a delightful hissing noise.

By this time dozens of other tourists had arrived to ride on the cranberry railroad.

"The train's a beaut!" Bert said to Jack.

From the silver wheels of the locomotive to the red caboose at the rear, the cranberry train was a riot of color. The engine and coal car were painted red, yellow, and blue. Behind them were three coaches, blue, red, and yellow.

Following these were four flatcars containing benches on either side.

"Where would you like to sit?" Mrs. Bobbsey asked as the twins and their friends crowded toward the train.

"How about the flatcars?" Nan suggested. "We can see more that way."

Freddie stopped for a moment to wave at the engineer, then with the others he climbed aboard the yellow flatcar. Seated on the long benches the children leaned forward to grasp the guard rail in front of them.

"All aboard!" cried the conductor. The last passengers took seats and the train started.

Flossie began to giggle. "It's saying chug, chug, glug, glug!"

"Here comes the conductor for our tickets," Nan told the others as a friendly looking man in railroad uniform walked down the outer edge of the car. As he punched their tickets, he said, smiling, "I hope you enjoy the trip. There are some surprises up ahead for you children."

"Surprises?" Flossie asked, her blue eyes widening. "What are they?"

"Be patient and you'll see," the conductor said as he moved away.

It was a breezy, sunny day and the Bobbseys breathed deeply of the sweet, fresh pine air as the train rumbled along. Soon the engine began to gather speed as it went down a small incline.

In a moment Freddie exclaimed, "I see one surprise!"

Leaning forward to glance down the tracks, the Bobbseys saw a miniature village situated in a green clearing. A tiny station had a white sign on it reading, "Peacedale Village."

The train slowed down.

"Hurray! Hurray! We're going to stop!" Freddie cried out.

"Oh, isn't it cute!" Flossie said, clapping her hands together and jumping up and down on the seat.

Peacedale Village was a charming, old-fashioned town of small buildings. A flagpole stood in the middle of the village green. Grouped around the edges of lush green grass were quaint structures. There was a church with a white spire, a general store, an inn, a mill with a real stream and paddle wheel, and four little houses.

When the train came to a halt the conductor stepped off, carrying an American flag in his hand. He walked directly to the flagpole and raised the flag to the top of it. As it fluttered in the breeze the passengers cheered.

While this was going on Freddie and Flossie had inched toward the steps of the flatcar. Before anyone could stop them they hopped to the ground. Seeing this, several other small children did the same. They ran across the grass to examine the lovely little buildings.

"Hey, come back here!" the conductor called, waving his arms. "You're not supposed to get off at this stop."

"Hey, come back here!"

he conductor called, waving his arms

But by this time the inquisitive little heads had poked into the buildings of Peacedale Village. Freddie and Flossie, hand in hand, walked through the general store. They did not hear the conductor. Then, joined by several other children, they scampered into the inn. People aboard the train chuckled as they watched the conductor trying to round up his young passengers.

"Come on, come on, all of you," the genial man said as he herded them back to the train.

The children climbed aboard a forward car, then started for their regular places. The conductor gave a signal. The cranberry locomotive went *toot toot* and started off.

In a few moments Freddie came to sit beside his mother. They had gone only a hundred yards farther when a startled look came into Mrs. Bobbsey's eyes. "Where's Flossie?" she asked.

"I don't know," Freddie answered. "I didn't see her after we came out of the inn."

"Then she's been left behind!" Mrs. Bobbsey cried out. "Conductor! Conductor!"

The trainman hurried to her side. "My little girl is still in Peacedale," she said.

The conductor signaled to the engineer with a wave of his hand. "We'll have to go back!"

With grinding wheels the train stopped. Then it began to back up slowly. When the caboose

came in sight of Peacedale Village, Mrs. Bobbsey gave a sigh of relief. Flossie was just coming
out of the tiny church.

Seeing the cranberry train backing up, she
dashed toward it. When it stopped, she hopped
aboard the yellow flatcar.

"Flossie! You gave us such a fright!" her
mother exclaimed.

"I'm sorry," the little girl said. "I was in the
church praying that we'd find Danny and the
bad man."

The conductor and several others smiled. He
moved on without saying another word.

Now the locomotive carried the visitors
through a woodsy section where pine trees grew
close to the tracks.

"Look at all the birdhouses!" Nan said as their
car went along. "I wonder why they put so many
there." Nearly every tree had one dangling from
a limb.

The next stop was Edaville Center. "Here's
where we will have some real fun!" said Jack
as they got off.

When Flossie stepped from the car, the conductor patted her golden curls and winked.
"Don't get lost," he whispered.

"I won't," she said, giggling. Then, as the
group stood on the pavement beside the track,
she said, "See what I found in the inn."

Flossie put her hand in her pocket and pulled out a small, black notebook. When Bert spied it he cried out in surprise, "Flossie, let me see that!"

He thumbed through the notebook. There was no identification, and its pages were empty.

"I'll bet this is Danny Rugg's!" Bert said.

Flossie asked why Danny had not written in it.

"I think he did," Bert told her. "In invisible ink."

Jack and Jane Hathaway were intrigued to hear this. "How can you tell whether it's written in invisible ink?" Jack questioned.

Bert asked his mother's permission to apply the heat test. This would require holding a lighted match beneath one of the pages.

"Maybe the book will tell where Danny and George are," he said.

When Mrs. Bobbsey gave her consent, Bert secured a packet of matches from a man passing by. Then, lighting a match, he held it under one of the blank pages.

Instantly a change began to take place on the paper. Writing, at first dim, became bolder. Eagerly the children waited to see what it would say.

CHAPTER XII

A RUNAWAY CAR

"LOOK what this says!" Bert cried excitedly.

The words that showed up were first a date, then beneath it were the words: *"They'll never know who did it."*

"What does that mean?" Freddie asked.

"I don't know," Bert answered. "I'll try some of the other pages. They may give the answer."

As the others looked on, Bert made the invisible writing appear on page after page. The second message said, *"I'm not the only one who took them. Got two new guns today."*

"That doesn't make sense," Jane said.

"I guess it's Danny's private code," Jack remarked.

The last writing which Bert's matches revealed read, *"We're going to Billy Goat C."*

"Goodness," Mrs. Bobbsey said. "This sounds like the language of a real criminal. Bert, do you really think the notebook belongs to Danny?"

"I'm sure this is his handwriting," her son answered. "The words have a hidden meaning. If we can figure them out, we'll find the boys."

As Bert carefully put the black notebook into his pocket, a call came over the loudspeakers posted here and there on the Edaville Center buildings.

"Come and get your barbecued chicken," a voice boomed. "It's served with delicious cranberry sauce."

Freddie sniffed the air. "I can smell it already," he said. "Boy, I'm hungry!"

Jack directed the Bobbseys to a long row of barbecue pits. Near by were several large tents, open on all sides. Under them were tables and chairs for the visitors.

After Mrs. Bobbsey had bought tickets for her group, each of them was served half a delicious chicken, dressing, and cranberry jelly. The group sat in the shade of the tents and ate their wonderful lunch.

How good everything tasted! As Freddie finished licking the tender meat off the drumstick, he asked Jack and Jane why there were so many birdhouses in the woods. A man sitting near them overheard the question and leaned toward Freddie.

"I'm a cranberry worker," he said. "I'll be

glad to tell you about it." He went on, "Do you know that both birds and bees help us to raise cranberries?"

"You mean they pick them?" Flossie asked.

The man chuckled. "Oh, no." Then he told the children that the birdhouses were built for swallows. In the evening the birds swept back and forth over the cranberry bogs, devouring the insects that might ruin the plants.

"Do the bees do that too?" Freddie asked.

Again the cranberry worker said no. Beehives were set on the edges of the bog to attract bees. As they flew from flower to flower to collect honey, pollen caught on their feet or wings and was transferred to other plants. "They save us a lot of work," the man concluded.

"Thank you for telling us," said Nan.

When she and the others finished eating, Jack said, "I want to show you a sleigh fire engine. Come on!"

Eagerly the others followed him to the exhibit building. Outside the door stood an old-fashioned automobile. Jack said this probably would be added to the exhibit inside.

"How high the seats are!" Bert said. He stepped onto the running board and sat down behind the wheel.

"You'd better get down from there," Mrs. Bobbsey warned him.

"Mother, these old cars don't run," Bert said. "They have to be cranked by hand in the front, and anyway they don't have any gas in them."

Jack had stepped to the front and spun the old crank. To everyone's amazement the motor caught.

Frightened, Bert reached his hand forward to try to turn it off. In doing so, his arm bumped into a lever. Without warning, the car started off!

Everyone cried out for Bert to stop it, but he did not know how. The old car headed straight for a cranberry bog!

"I mustn't go in there!" Bert thought wildly.

He clung to the big steering wheel and honked loudly as he drove the car around in circles. Visitors scampered off as the boy dodged this way and that, avoiding trees and buildings.

The commotion brought the curator of the museum running out of the building. Seeing what was happening, he thought Bert was just having fun and told him to stop the car.

"I can't! I don't know how!" Bert screamed.

The curator shouted directions, but the noise of the chugging engine was so great that Bert could not hear him.

Frantically the boy put his foot on what he thought was the brake. It did not work. Neither did the old emergency lever.

Suddenly Bert noticed a small knoll and headed for it. Driving up the grassy slope he hoped the car would stall. It did. Giving a final loud backfire, the engine stopped and the car rolled back down the hill to a standstill. Bert hopped out. He was shaking.

"It was all my fault," said Jack and told the curator about cranking the motor.

"It's just as much my fault," said the man, who was short and bald. "I shouldn't have left the magneto turned on."

The man said the car had been left outside temporarily, to be put into the museum later that day.

"Congratulations for your quick thinking, young man," he said to Bert. "Otherwise there might have been an accident."

He took charge of the car. The Bobbseys and their friends entered the museum to see the models on display.

Freddie was overjoyed at the hundreds of model trains of all sizes. One that intrigued him was an old car mounted on train wheels. Nan read the sign standing before the exhibit. It said the old auto train had been used in Maine for many years.

"When I get home," said Freddie, "I'm going to ask Dad to put train wheels on our car."

This made Mrs. Bobbsey laugh. "What happened to Dad's little fat fireman, Freddie?" she asked. "Do you want to become an engineer now?"

Freddie was thoughtful for a moment, then he said he would stick to being a fireman. He liked his father's nickname for him. Mr. Bobbsey sometimes called Flossie his fat fairy, and she too had missed hearing her nickname on this trip.

"There are some old fire engines on display in the next room," Jack said. "Come on, I'll show them to you, Freddie."

The little boy's eyes grew large as he gazed at two rows of ancient fire engines. They were steamers and pumpers.

"And look here, Bert!" he cried, running toward the end of the building. "There's the sleigh fire engine." It stood on sleigh runners, and Jack said it had been drawn by horses and was for fighting fires in snowy weather.

"I'm going to build one of these next winter," Freddie said.

After looking at everything in the museum, Mrs. Bobbsey suggested that they visit the curio shop. "I understand cranberry candy is on sale."

"Oh, goody, let's get some!" Flossie urged.

The curio shop was near by. On display were cranberry scoops of various sizes.

Bert and Nan drew aside from the others and

whispered for a few moments. Then, pooling their money, they bought their mother a decorative birchwood scoop. Inside was a small container for holding flowers or ivy.

"Thank you so much, my dears," Mrs. Bobbsey said, hugging the older twins.

"Oh, look, here are the cranberry lollipops!" Flossie cried.

Mrs. Bobbsey bought both pops and candy sticks for all the children.

"I guess the only thing left to see is the movie about cranberry growing," Jane said. "Want to see it?"

"If the birds and bees are in it," said Flossie.

The Bobbseys and their friends went into the building in which the movies were being shown. They watched as the narrator explained that in this part of the country most of the harvesting was done by hand. Pickers would comb the scoops through the bushes, gathering the cranberries and dumping them into boxes.

At one point Flossie said aloud, "Here's the part about the birds." They watched as the movie showed workers erecting birdhouses atop long poles in the middle of the bogs.

All at once Nan nudged her brother. She leaned close to him and whispered, "I think I have that notebook figured out, Bert."

"What do you mean?"

"Come on outside, and I'll tell you," his sister said.

The picture was nearly over so the twins slipped quietly from their seats and went out in the bright sunlight. Bert took the notebook from his pocket, and Nan pointed out the date of the first serious message.

" 'They'll never know who did it,' " she said, "is the very day I was frightened by the ghost when we were sleeping on the porch."

"That's right, sis," Bert said excitedly.

Nan turned several pages, then said, "There are two different messages with the same date. One says, 'I'm not the only one who took some,' and the other says, 'Got two new guns today.' Bert, that was the same day the fusees and torpedoes were stolen!"

"That's swell! Good for you!" Bert praised his sister's deduction. "I suppose Danny meant someone else took fusees too. I wonder if he knows who it was."

"I'll bet it was the man with the black bag," Nan said excitedly.

Bert agreed this was probably true. Then he said, "Have you figured out the one about Billy Goat C, Nan?"

The girl admitted that this had her baffled.

"Anyway," she said, "according to the last date, Danny was here yesterday."

Bert surmised that he might not be far away. Just then the movies let out, and the train pulled into the station for anyone wanting a ride back to Cranberry Junction.

"Let's ask the engineer if he has seen Danny and George," Nan suggested.

The twins hurried to where the engineer stood beside the coal car, waiting for the signal to start. Bert asked, "Did you see two boys roaming around here who didn't seem to be with anyone else?"

"Yes, this morning."

"Where, sir?"

"Not far from here," the engineer replied. "We've been on the lookout for those fellows after hearing from the Plymouth police. But we haven't been able to catch them."

The engineer said he would continue to look for the two runaways.

"We'll do the same," Bert said, and thanked the engineer for his information.

Then they all got on the train. As it chugged back toward Cranberry Junction the Bobbseys cast glances in all directions over the cranberry bogs. There was no sign of Danny and George.

Suddenly the quietness of the place was shaken by a tremendous explosion.

Somebody yelled, "The locomotive has exploded!"

CHAPTER XIII

GHOST WALK

AFTER the explosion, the train stopped and everybody jumped off. Bert and Nan were among the first to race up alongside the locomotive. Nothing had happened to it, and the engineer was just stepping from the cab.

"What made the noise?" Bert asked.

"Somebody must have put a torpedo on the rail," the man replied.

Bert snapped his fingers. "That proves it!" he exclaimed.

"Proves what?" the engineer said.

Bert told him that the boys he had seen that morning must have been Danny and George. "My sister and I think that Danny took two torpedoes from the train to Boston."

"And used one to stop this train," Nan added.

"That's not a very funny prank," the engineer said, annoyed. "The sooner those young mischief makers are caught, the better."

The conductor shouted "All aboard!" and the passengers went back to their seats. After two toots of the whistle the cranberry railroad locomotive puffed off again toward the junction. As the train neared the station it let out two more mournful whistles.

"As soon as we get there," Freddie said, "you'd better call the policemen, Bert, and tell them about Danny and George."

"And tell George's parents, too," Flossie said. "They must be terribly worried about those two naughty boys."

When the train arrived, Bert ran inside the station and went to a telephone booth. First he called Plymouth police headquarters. He told the lieutenant at the desk what had happened at Edaville.

"I'll send men right out there to search for the missing boys," the lieutenant promised.

After hanging up, Bert put in a call to the Rench home. George's mother answered.

"Oh, I have been so worried," she said after hearing Bert's story. "I do hope now that they'll come home."

"Perhaps they'll set off the other torpedo first," Bert suggested. "I'm sure that Danny had two of them."

"He did," Mrs. Rench replied.

When Bert asked her how she knew, George's

mother was silent for a moment. Then she said, "That's the reason the boys ran away."

Not understanding what she meant, Bert asked if she would explain. Mrs. Rench said that Danny and George had set off a torpedo in the cellar.

"Dad and I thought the house had blown up," Mrs. Rench said, almost in tears. "Fortunately the boys were not hurt, but they were so afraid of being punished that they ran off."

"I see," said Bert and thought as he hung up, "That's just like Danny!"

When he reported this news to the others, Mrs. Bobbsey sighed with relief. She said she was happy that both railroad guns had been fired off without doing any harm.

"Yes, but George and Danny are afraid to go home," Nan remarked. "What's going to happen to them?"

Mrs. Bobbsey said she felt sure the boys would soon be found and brought home. As she led the way to the car, Flossie called out:

"I'm thirsty."

"Me too," Freddie chimed in.

"I'd say we all are," Mrs. Bobbsey said, smiling. "What would you like to drink?"

Bert said that ice cold cranberry juice was being sold at a counter inside the station. "That's what I want," he added.

They all went in and ordered a cup apiece.
How delicious it tasted!

Their thirst quenched, the Bobbseys and their
friends got into the station wagon and soon were
on their way back to Plymouth. Mrs. Bobbsey
delivered the car to Mrs. Hathaway and
thanked her for the use of it.

Meanwhile, the twins had gone into Aunt
Nan's house. Seeing her face they guessed that
another surprise was in store for them.

"How did you make out?" she asked.

After hearing about the exciting time at Edaville, Miss Shaw said, "We've just received a
wonderful invitation. The Woodsons have invited us to dinner this evening and want us to
stay overnight on Clark's Island."

"Oh, how wonderful!" Nan exclaimed. "And
Jack and Jane, too?"

"They're included," her aunt replied, smiling. "I've told Mrs. Hathaway about it."

She went on to say that Mary Jo's mother
would meet them all at the town dock at six
o'clock in her large motorboat.

"I didn't know they had a boat," Bert remarked. "That's nifty."

That evening at six o'clock sharp the Bobbseys
and their friends were waiting at the dock.
They waved to Mrs. Woodson as she steered her
sleek craft in for a landing. Bert and Nan helped

their elderly aunt down the steep ramp and assisted her into the boat. Then they introduced their mother, and everyone climbed aboard.

Mrs. Woodson backed away from the pier. Then, with full speed ahead, she guided the craft past the channel markers on the way to Clark's Island. The sun sent slanting rays across the beautiful harbor.

Suddenly Bert said, "Look at that speedboat! Wow, it's fast!"

The craft, a hundred yards on their starboard side, soon shot ahead.

Without warning, it suddenly veered left and crossed in front of their bow. The wake caused large waves. The Woodson boat bounced through them, making a loud slapping sound.

"My, that was a dangerous thing to do!" Aunt Nan remarked.

"It certainly was," Mrs. Woodson agreed. "I wonder who that man could be?"

As she spoke the speedboat turned about and cut across their bow again.

"He's certainly making it tough for us," Mrs. Bobbsey said.

"Do you think he's trying to scare us, Mother?" Nan asked.

"Maybe he's just teasing," Flossie said.

Mrs. Woodson said that if the rude fellow was trying to frighten them, he was certainly wasting his time. "You'll get to Clark's Island on sched-ule," she said with determination, "because Mother has dinner waiting for us."

The driver of the speedboat did not try the trick again. He disappeared in the distance. Skillfully Mrs. Woodson followed the channel and landed at a dock some distance east of her cottage.

"Now I know why we didn't see your boat be-fore," Bert remarked. "We didn't come this far with Mr. Donald."

Bert and Jack hopped ashore first and tied the boat. Then the party walked along a path to the bungalow.

Mary Jo ran out to meet them. "Guess what?" she said after she had been introduced to Mrs. Bobbsey. "We're going to play ghost walk to-night."

"That'll be fun," Freddie said. "If you're a ghost, Mother, may I catch you?"

Mrs. Bobbsey replied with a wink, "Yes, if you can find me." She often played games with her children and sometimes surprised them by winning.

Mary Jo's grandmother greeted her guests cordially. Then, after chatting a few moments, they all sat down to dinner.

New England clam chowder was served first. This was followed by a savory lobster dish.

Grandmother Woodson said that the recipe had been her great-grandmother's.

"Lobsters must have been in the world a long time," said Flossie. "Were they in Noah's Ark?"

"I suppose they were," Grandmother Woodson replied, smiling.

By the time the delicious meal had ended it was growing dusk. "There's only a sliver of a moon tonight," Jane noted, "so it'll be real spooky for playing ghost walk."

Aunt Nan and Grandmother Woodson thought they were too old to go prowling about with sheets over them. It was decided that Mary Jo's mother and Mrs. Bobbsey would be the ghosts.

"But we should have one more," Mary Jo said. "Then the game won't be over so soon."

Jack suggested that Mr. Cook, their neighbor, be called in to be the third ghost. This suggestion was accepted, and the boy hurried off to bring him.

When he arrived the twins noted that Mr. Cook was very short and had dark hair and a small black mustache.

Jane whispered to Nan, "He's small for a grown-up ghost, don't you think?"

"Maybe he can use a single-size sheet," Nan replied, giggling.

The Woodsons had several discarded sheets

they used for the game. After Mr. Cook and the two women had been draped as ghosts, Grandmother Woodson said to them, "You'll have a five-minute start on the children."

The three ghosts bowed and without a word hurried off into the darkness. After the minutes had passed, the twins, together with Jack and Jane, went in pursuit of the grownups.

"Let's take Tui with us," Flossie suggested.

Mary Jo laughed. "That wouldn't be fair. Tui would find them right away."

"But—but it's very dark out there," the little girl reminded the others.

"That's what makes it fun," Jane said. "Don't be afraid, Flossie."

"Oh, she's not afraid," Freddie spoke up, defending his twin. "Flossie just likes dogs."

Nan took her sister's hand while Bert grabbed Freddie's. Grandmother Woodson provided Bert and Jack with flashlights in case the children got lost.

"But don't use them unless you have to," she said. "It's one of the rules of the game."

"This way up the trail," Mary Jo called out, and the children made their way cautiously along the darkened path.

Every so often they would stop and listen. Once Nan thought she heard a giggle.

"That sounds like Mother!" she whispered.

"Woo! Woo!" exclaimed the ghost

The Bobbseys crept quietly to the spot from which the noise had come. All at once a figure jumped out at them. "Woo! Woo!" exclaimed the ghost.

The four Bobbseys grabbed at the white sheet. "Mother, it's only you!" Flossie said, and pulled the sheet off her mother's head.

"We've caught a ghost! We've caught a ghost!" Freddie called out gleefully, jumping up and down.

"Now you'll have to help us find the rest of the ghosts, Mother," Nan said.

Creeping stealthily along, the children suddenly heard a little sneeze. Jack and Jane dashed forward. Just then another white-sheeted figure jumped out at them.

"Boo!" it exclaimed.

Once captured, the ghost proved to be Mrs. Woodson.

"Isn't this fun?" said Flossie as the sheet was removed.

"It sure is," Freddie said. "Who's afraid of ghosts, anyway?"

The party had not gone much farther when a small ghost leaped in front of them, waving his arms.

"I've got you, Mr. Cook!" Bert said, wrapping his arms around the sheeted figure.

"I give up," came Mr. Cook's voice.

"Hurray! Hurray! We've caught all the ghosts!" Freddie declared.

With laughter and giggles the children started back toward the Woodson cottage. Suddenly Bert heard rustling in the bushes to his left. He stopped for a moment as the others continued on. He was about to reach into his pocket for his flashlight when another ghost jumped out at him!

"But there couldn't be a fourth ghost!" Bert thought, his heart pounding.

The figure leaped on the boy, pinning him to the ground. Then the sheeted head bent close and hissed into his ear:

"Get off Clark's Island and don't come back!"

CHAPTER XIV

A TELLTALE CAMPFIRE

"LET me go!" Bert cried out.

The wiry lad grappled fiercely with his heavier opponent. As the two rolled on the ground Bert suddenly grasped the sheet and pulled it off. The fellow muttered something, jumped up and dashed into the woods.

Bert played his flashlight on the fleeing figure, but the man dodged out of sight before the boy could catch more than a glimpse of him.

Having heard Bert's shout, the others came running back. Learning what had happened, Mary Jo said, "Now we know there really is somebody masquerading as a ghost on Clark's Island!"

Bert wanted to continue chasing the man, but his mother thought they should get more help before doing this. "I'm sure Mr. Cook can take care of it."

Mr. Cook said he hoped so, then went home to call his neighbors and make the search. The others returned to the Woodson cottage.

As they were preparing for bed, the children discussed the ghost and the red glow they had seen in the sky the evening before.

"Did you see it?" Nan asked Mary Jo.

"Yes. People here went to see about it but couldn't find the person who lit it."

"Was it a railroad flare?" Nan questioned.

"We think so," Mary Jo replied. "The ghost must have lighted it."

"And then went off in a boat," Nan guessed.

After everyone was in bed Tui started growling in the kitchen. Bert roused Jack.

"Let's sneak out and see if anybody's prowling around the house," he suggested.

The boys quietly went into the hall. Just then Nan came from her room. In the darkness the three whispered a plan. Nan would keep Tui in the house so the snooper would not be warned away. The boys would scout around and capture the ghost.

"The two of us can surely catch him," said Bert.

Silently opening the kitchen door, they tiptoed out and crept around the house. All at once they heard someone walking along the path toward the cottage.

Bending low to avoid detection, the boys waited. Now a man was directly in front of them.

"Get him!" Bert shouted, and the boys jumped on the figure.

Jack applied a vise-like grip to the man's legs while Bert secured a head lock. The stranger was wrestled to the ground, and Bert plunked himself on the man's mid-section.

"Ugh! Um! Let me up!" he pleaded, trying to get his breath.

"Who are you?" Bert demanded.

"Mack—Mack Donald, the harbor master."

"Oh, no!" Bert exclaimed, getting up.

The noise had alerted the entire household except Freddie and Flossie. Lights flashed on, and a beam streaming from one of the windows cut across the figure of the prone prisoner.

"It *is* Mack!" Jack yelled.

"Who did you think it was?" Mr. Donald said wryly. "A ghost?"

"Yes!" said Bert. "I'm sorry." He told the story of the ghost in the woods.

When the harbor master stood up and brushed himself off, he chuckled at his predicament. "You fellows ought to join the police force," he said.

"Come on inside," Bert invited him. "Tell us why you're here."

Seated in the living room, Mack explained that he had come quietly tonight to investigate the ghost.

"Mr. Cook is doing that," Nan told him.

Mack ran to the neighbor's house and learned the men had not found the ghost. When he returned he said, "I'll continue the search."

"Please let me help you," Bert begged.

"And me," said Nan, Jack, and Jane together.

Mack looked toward Mrs. Bobbsey. "I'd like to take them. They could be a big help."

Mrs. Bobbsey gave her consent for them to join in the search. "But on one condition. I'm going with you!"

It was decided that the best plan would be for Mrs. Bobbsey and the harbor master each to lead a search party but to keep reasonably close together.

"If either of us gets into trouble," Mack said, "we'll give a crow call to the other party."

Mrs. Bobbsey selected Bert, Jack, and Nan in her group. Mack would take Mary Jo and Jane with him. Aunt Nan would stay with the small twins.

"But leave Tui here on guard," she requested.

"All right," said Mary Jo.

Equipping themselves with flashlights, the

two parties set off about one hundred yards apart. Bert shone his light only when it was necessary to track his way through the heavy underbrush.

"Mother, you're sure game to hunt for a ghost," her son said admiringly.

"I'd like to catch him myself," she said with a chuckle.

Now and then the Bobbseys heard Mack and his group pushing through the scrubby woodland.

Suddenly an eerie "hoo-hoo" came from a low limb near Nan's head. The girl froze with fright. But an instant later she realized that it was only an owl, and sighed in relief.

After they had walked along another ten minutes, Jack whispered, "Bert, out with your light!"

Bert obeyed. "What's up?"

"A small light ahead!"

"I see it now, too," Mrs. Bobbsey said.

"Let's creep up quietly and surround the place," Bert suggested.

Crouching low, the searchers stepped gingerly across the ground. Before them was a low campfire flickering in the blackness. Two men sat around it. The tongues of flame caused weird shadows to play across their faces.

Nan whispered in her mother's ear, "One of

them is the tall fellow we saw on the train! The man who tried to sell you some antiques!"

"The other man," Bert said in a low tone, "is the one who tried to scare us with his motor-

boat when we were coming to Clark's Island."

"Trying to keep us from visiting, no doubt," Mrs. Bobbsey whispered back, gazing intently at the shorter fellow.

The men began to talk. "Okay, Lanky," the

shorter one said. "It'll be a perfect time to help ourselves to some more antiques."

"Sure, Cracky. Everybody'll be watching that Pilgrim parade, and we can sneak in easy."

So these men were the thieves, the watchers thought. And they were planning another robbery!

What should the Bobbseys and Jack do now? Should they run up and try to seize the men? Or call to Mack for help?

Mrs. Bobbsey whispered that if these fellows were criminals they might injure the children in an outright attack. It was decided that Bert should give Mack the warning signal.

Cupping his hands, Bert cried, "Caw, caw!"

Lanky looked up worriedly. Cracky mocked him. "Don't get so jumpy," he said. "Just because that kid frightened you off when you were playing ghost, you're a bundle of nerves."

Lanky sneered and said, "He won't get away so easy next time. We'll frighten everybody off this island and keep it for our headquarters!"

Bert and Nan hoped that Mack had heard the crow call. How long could they crouch in the darkness waiting for him without giving away their position?

And what about the two thieves? Would they remain at the campfire or go to their boat?

Jack Hathaway shifted his weight from one

foot to the other. Snap! He had stepped on a twig.

This time both men looked startled. "Hey, someone's spying on us!" Lanky said.

"I told you to be more careful with those flares!" Cracky hissed. "The harbor cops and the Coast Guard are probably after us now. Well, don't just sit there. Let's get out of here!"

Jumping to their feet, the two men dashed off toward the beach.

CHAPTER XV

TREASURE IN THE SAND

AS the two mysterious men sped toward the shore, the Bobbsey twins gave crow calls loud and clear. A second later they heard a reply from someone close at hand.

"Mack! Mack!" Bert yelled out. "Follow us!"

He and the others had already started after the thieves.

"Here we come!" the harbor master cried out and was soon on their heels with his party.

In a moment they saw two flashlights bobbing far ahead. Then the beams disappeared from sight. The sound of a motorboat broke the stillness of the night.

"We've lost them!" Nan wailed.

Mack called out to the thieves, "Stop! Stop in the name of the law!"

But Lanky and Cracky had no intention of

stopping. Instead they increased the speed of their motor and in a few seconds were far out on the water.

"I'll alert the police," Mack said. "See you in the morning."

He ran off, and the others went back to the Woodsons'.

"I hope those awful men get caught before they can come here again," said Mary Jo.

Next morning as they were finishing breakfast Mack came to the house. He said the police had found the thieves' boat and were holding it. But the men had disappeared.

Mack smiled. "The police wanted me to thank you for your sleuthing," he said. "And especially for finding out that the men's nicknames are Lanky and Cracky. And now, how would you like to do a little hunting with me?"

"That would be keen," said Bert. "You mean hunt for buried antiques, maybe?"

"Exactly."

"I want to be a detective too," said Freddie.

"And me," Flossie insisted.

"All right."

The harbor master and his young friends hurried first to the site of the thieves' campfire. Tui bounded along with them.

"We'll look for freshly dug holes in this area," he suggested.

Every inch of ground for yards around was thoroughly examined, but nowhere was there evidence of fresh digging.

"How about following the men's trail to the waterfront?" Bert said. "Maybe we'll find something where their boat was hidden."

"I want to stay here," Freddie spoke up. He and Flossie were busy digging in a sandy spot near the campfire. "We might find a treasure."

"All right," said Mack with a grin. "Call out if you reach it before we get back."

With Tui bounding ahead, the rest of the searchers fanned out. Some walked on the freshly made trail, the others on either side.

"If the loot is hidden anywhere along here we should find it," Mack said.

But all the way down to the beach there was not the slightest trace of any hidden antiques.

All at once Mary Jo cried out, "Look! I see where they hid the boat!"

The children ran to a spot near the water line where an old tree had toppled over. Mary Jo said it had been felled by a hurricane several years before. Gnarled branches had made a little canopy over a tiny inlet of water. Freshly cut green boughs had been interlaced among the dead branches.

"No wonder people couldn't spot the boat from the water," Bert said.

"Pretty clever," Mack agreed.

The little group searched the spot well, but still they found nothing.

Bert suggested that they tear off the camouflage of boughs and make a search. The children did this in a hurry. Now the sun streamed through the dead branches.

"I see something down there in the water!" Jack cried out.

He kicked off his loafers and waded to the spot. On the gravelly bottom three feet beneath the surface lay a red object. He picked it up and showed it to the others.

"Wow!" Bert exclaimed. "It's a fusee!"

"Now we know for sure Lanky stole the flares from the train," said Nan. "It means too that Danny Rugg didn't take them."

Mack took the fusee. "I'll destroy this later. You know, these things will burn under water as well as in the open air."

Just then the searchers were startled by high-pitched shouts. "That's Freddie!" Nan exclaimed with a worried look, wondering if Lanky and Cracky had returned when the others were not watching.

"Golly, I hope they're not in trouble," Bert said, dashing toward the place where they had left the younger twins.

Breaking into the clearing, Bert and Nan

saw that Freddie and Flossie were alone. The little boy was lying flat on his stomach. One arm extended deep into a hole.

Flossie was standing beside him, jumping up and down in excitement. "We found something!" she called to the others. "Come here quick and help us!"

Bert, Nan, and the others crowded about the younger twins. Freddie made way for his brother, who reached down and grabbed something made of metal.

Tugging at it several times, he finally

loosened the object from the sandy soil. Bert held it up for everyone to examine.

"It looks like a blade," Jack said.

The rusty bit of metal about three feet long intrigued Mack. "Say, that looks like the business end of a sword," he declared.

Bert and Jack scraped the sand and chunks of earth off the blade. Nan bent close to examine it. "There's writing on it!" she said. "Look here!"

By tracing each letter carefully, they could make out the letters, "C-h-a-m-p-l-a-i-n."

"Champlain!" Nan shouted.

"And look at this date!" Bert declared. In smaller writing were the numbers, "1605."

"What a discovery!" Mack said, taking the blade in his hands and turning it over and over.

Suddenly Freddie's mouth opened, and his eyes widened as a thought struck him. "Maybe —maybe it goes with the handle!"

"You mean the one at the old Warren house?" Nan asked him.

"Yes."

"But how would the handle be there and the blade here?" said Jack.

"Let's take it to Mr. Warren and see if it fits the handle," Freddie urged.

"That would be a good idea," said Mack, adding that he had once seen a map of the Plymouth area which had been made by the famous French explorer, Champlain. "So you might be right, Freddie, because it's suspected the hilt in the museum might have belonged to him."

Taking the old blade with them, the Bobbseys and their friends made their way back to Mary Jo's house. The twins wanted to leave at once, but the Woodsons urged them to stay to luncheon.

"Let's have a swim and a picnic lunch over on Saquish Head," Mary Jo proposed. Her mother seconded the invitation, and Mrs. Bobbsey accepted for the group. Fortunately all the visitors had brought swim suits, and put them on.

In half an hour they set off in the motorboat. Soon they were streaking across the water.

"Maybe Lanky and Cracky are hiding there," Bert whispered to Jack. "Let's hunt for them."

"Okay."

When they reached a small dock, the two boys hopped out and tied the craft to a metal ring on the dock.

"I'm first in the water," cried Freddie, running into the surf and making a shallow dive. Flossie followed him, then Mrs. Bobbsey and Mrs. Woodson.

The older children decided to explore a little before going for a swim.

"I'll show you the site of the old fort," Mary Jo said.

About two hundred feet away they saw all that remained of the ancient fortification. There were the crumbling remains of old walls and several deep depressions in the ground.

Nan wandered off to explore a low spot next to a sandy hummock. All at once she let out a cry and disappeared.

"What happened to her?" Jane asked, terrified.

"She fell into a hole!" Bert shouted, running to his sister's assistance.

"I'm all right, I'm all right!" Nan called up from a deep pit into which she had fallen. The thin layer of sod which had grown over the opening had given way. Nan and the soft turf had landed at the bottom.

"What's down there?" her twin asked as he bent down and extended a hand to haul his sister up.

"Bert," Nan cried excitedly, "there's something like a tunnel leading from this pit! This would be a wonderful hiding place for stolen things."

"Let's explore it!" Jack said eagerly.

"Sure thing," Bert replied. He let himself

down into the hole, followed by the others.

Stepping carefully into the black passage-way, Bert felt his way along.

"We should have brought flashlights," the boy said.

All of a sudden Bert stepped into a pool of icy water chest high. He scrambled back in a hurry.

"We can't go any farther than this," he said. "Too dangerous."

"If it's a tunnel maybe we can find the other end of it," said Jane.

Bert stood on Jack's shoulders and raised himself to the top of the pit. Then he helped the others out. The children ran here and there looking for another opening but found none.

Finally Nan said, "Let's come back here to-morrow with flashlights and see if we can get beyond the water Bert stepped in."

"Yes," Jane agreed. "And now we'd better go for our swim."

It was two o'clock when the picnickers pulled away from Saquish Head. The visitors would change clothes at the Woodson cottage, then go back to Plymouth.

They moored the craft and started up the path toward the cottage. Grandma Woodson and Aunt Nan came down to the beach to meet them.

"I think I've solved a mystery for you," Mary Jo's grandmother said, her eyes twinkling.

"About the ghost?" Nan asked.

"No."

"Lanky and Cracky?"

"No."

"Who then? I give up."

Grandmother Woodson's answer amazed everyone. "I think I know where Danny and George are."

CHAPTER XVI

FIRE FIGHTERS

"DO you really know where Danny and George are hiding?" Bert spoke up.

"I believe so," Grandmother Woodson replied with a chuckle.

"Did somebody tell you?" Nan asked.

"No. I figured it out myself."

"Please, Grandma, tell us where they are!" Mary Jo said impatiently.

"I believe you'll find them at Billington Sea," the elderly woman declared.

Judging from the puzzled expressions on the Bobbseys' faces, Mary Jo realized that the visitors had never heard of Billington Sea.

"It's a pond west of Plymouth," she told them. Then she turned to her grandmother. "What makes you think they're at Billington Sea?" she asked.

Aunt Nan answered. "Mrs. Woodson deciphered Danny's coded message," she said.

"Which one?" Bert asked.

"The one about Billy Goat C," Aunt Nan went on. "Danny must have heard about John Billington, who came over on the 'Mayflower.' "

"Oh, I get it," Bert said. "Danny wanted to disguise the name of the pond, so he gave it a nickname."

Grandmother Woodson smiled and nodded. "That's my guess," she said as they started back toward the cottage. "It wouldn't surprise me if the Bobbseys found Danny and George there."

"Let's go right now!" Flossie urged as she ran along the path.

On the way to the cottage the children told Grandmother Woodson and Aunt Nan about their adventure at Saquish.

"Gracious me!" Aunt Nan exclaimed. "These nieces and nephews of mine are making detectives out of all of us!"

"Especially me," Grandmother Woodson said, chuckling, as she climbed the steps to the porch of her home.

The Bobbseys and Hathaways quickly changed from their bathing suits to sports clothing. Then Mrs. Bobbsey said, "I think we'd better leave right away. And thank you for a most pleasant visit."

"I'm glad you enjoyed it." Grandmother Woodson smiled. "And I do hope you find those boys at Billington Sea."

Mrs. Bobbsey promised to take the twins to the pond that afternoon. "And if we find Danny and George," she added, "the credit is all yours, Grandma Woodson."

Mary Jo and Tui stayed with her, while the others hurried toward the beach. Freddie tucked the old sword blade through his belt and held his head high as he marched along the path.

"Look! He thinks he's Champlain!" Nan giggled.

Overhearing the remark, Freddie answered, *"Oui, oui."*

They all took their places in Mrs. Woodson's motorboat and after a breezy ride across Plymouth Harbor, arrived at the town dock.

"Good luck to you," Mrs. Woodson said as her guests stepped out of the boat.

They all called out their thanks as Mrs. Woodson turned her boat about and headed back toward Clark's Island.

As the Bobbseys and their friends started toward North Street, Jane said, "Will you please excuse Jack and me? We have to hurry along for our music lesson."

"Oh, really?" Nan asked. "What are you studying?"

"Piano."

"I can play Chopsticks!" Freddie said.

"Me too," Flossie piped up. "Freddie is one chopstick, and I'm the other!"

The Hathaways laughed. Then Mrs. Bobbsey said, "Of course, we'll excuse you, Jack and Jane. You mustn't be late for your lesson."

"I'm sure Mother will want you to take our car and go to Billington Sea," Jane said. "I don't think she's using it this afternoon."

"That would be very nice," Mrs. Bobbsey replied.

"Let us know if you find Danny and George," Jack called as he and Jane ran toward home.

The twins might have raced along with them, but they thought it polite to stay with their mother and Aunt Nan, who walked more slowly.

"Oh dear, I can't get along as fast as I used to," Aunt Nan complained.

Freddie spoke up. "Aunt Nan, suppose you and Flossie and I stop in to see Mr. Warren while the others go ahead for the car."

"Fine," Mrs. Bobbsey said. "We'll meet you in front of his house."

She and the older twins walked on ahead. The

younger ones, skipping beside Aunt Nan, turned into the walk leading to the old house.

"Come on in," Mr. Warren greeted them.

"Look what I found!" Freddie said as he pulled the blade from his belt.

"Well, well, what's this?" the custodian asked. "Are you playing a new game?"

"No. We found it! We found it!" Flossie said.

"And we think it fits the handle!" Freddie went on.

Mr. Warren was puzzled by the children's chatter until Aunt Nan explained their find.

"This *is* a surprise!" Mr. Warren said. "Wait here until I fetch the handle."

He disappeared into his office and returned with the gold-flecked antique. Then as the children and Aunt Nan watched breathlessly, he fitted the two pieces together.

"By George!" Mr. Warren exclaimed. "They fit! Exactly! But—but how did the blade get to Clark's Island?"

"Somebody took it there," Flossie said.

Mr. Warren bobbed his head. "That could be! Someone who did not know the value of the old blade."

"Now Champlain can have his sword again," Freddie remarked.

Mr. Warren said it was too late for Champlain. But perhaps present-day people could be treated to the sight of the rare old relic.

"You keep it," Flossie said.

"Yes!" Freddie agreed. "We want you to have it for your museum."

"Thank you," Mr. Warren said, "if that meets with your mother's approval."

Aunt Nan said she was certain Mrs. Bobbsey would be more than glad to leave the Champlain blade at Plymouth. "This is where it belongs," she said.

Just then the horn of the Hathaway station wagon sounded in front of the building.

"Good-by," Flossie said to Mr. Warren. "We're going to Nanny Goat Sea."

"Oh," Freddie said, "Flossie gets everything all mixed up, Mr. Warren. We're going to Billy Goat Ocean."

"Billington Sea!" Aunt Nan explained. She and Mr. Warren chuckled.

When Aunt Nan reached the car with the children, she said she would go home and prepare the evening meal. "I hope you find those two young runaways," she said, "and bring them back to Plymouth."

She gave Mrs. Bobbsey directions, and the searchers set off. After driving several miles Bert spied a sign and cried out, "We're coming to Billington Sea, Mother."

Soon they were driving through a pine woods. Just as the pond came into view Freddie exclaimed, "Look! I see smoke!"

"Where?" Bert asked.

"Over there," the little boy said, pointing.

"Jeepers! It's a brush fire. And it's getting bigger," Bert exclaimed.

"It certainly is gaining headway," Mrs. Bobbsey remarked as clouds of smoke billowed into the air.

"I must tell Chief Holt," Freddie announced.

"I wonder where we can find a telephone," his mother said.

"I see a house," Flossie replied. "Right over there." An old farmhouse stood at the end of a long lane leading from the highway. Mrs. Bobbsey turned into it.

"Oh, I hope someone's at home," Nan said.

"May I make the call?" Freddie asked, " 'cause the chief is my friend."

"All right. But hurry," replied his mother.

Freddie got out of the car, ran up to the house, and knocked on the door. A woman answered it. When she heard Freddie's report she quickly ushered him in, and the little boy telephoned the fire chief at Plymouth.

"We'll be right over there," Chief Holt said upon hearing the message.

"Will you bring your trailer boat, too?" Freddie asked.

"Of course. But why?"

"I have a feeling you might need it," Freddie replied.

"All right, lieutenant," the chief said. "Stand by!"

Freddie hung up, thanked the woman and hurried back to the car. Mrs. Bobbsey drove off. When they reached the main road again they could see that the fire had made rapid strides.

"Let's stay here and wait for the fire engines," Freddie coaxed.

"I don't think we should," his mother said. "We ought to look for Danny and George immediately. They might get into more mischief."

"Perhaps," Nan added, "they should be warned about the fire."

Mrs. Bobbsey drove toward the shore of the pond, and the twins looked left and right in search of the runaways.

"Goodness! Look what's ahead!" Mrs. Bobbsey exclaimed. Brush on either side of the road was burning fiercely. A tree had caught fire, and embers were falling onto the road.

"I'll have to back up," the twins' mother said.

Putting the gear into reverse, she had gone less than a hundred feet when Freddie cried out, "Mother, the fire's in back of us too!"

"Oh dear!" Nan cried out. "We're trapped!"

Mrs. Bobbsey ordered the children to get out of the car. They hurried to the waterfront.

"If we have to," Bert said, "we can all get into the water to keep from being burned."

"Oh, I hope it's not that bad!" Nan cried.

Just then the Bobbseys heard sirens in the distance. "The firemen are coming!" Freddie cried excitedly.

"Hurray for the chief!" Flossie said. "He'll rescue us."

Three fire trucks and the chief's car appeared on the road. One pulled up in front of the Bobbsey car, and two stopped beside it. Immediately firemen hopped off the apparatus. Four men carried tanks of chemical extinguishers on their backs and started to use them at once.

Swish, swish. The chemical began to put out part of the blaze.

Men from the third engine, a pumper, laid a hose into the water of Billington Sea, and the pumper began to throw a strong stream among the burning trees.

"I wish I had my pumper here," Freddie remarked.

The crackle of the fire and the hissing of the wet embers fascinated the children. After a few minutes Nan said breathlessly, "They have it under control!"

"We sure do," declared Chief Holt, as he walked over to where they were standing. "Thanks for giving us the alarm. Lieutenant Freddie deserves a medal!"

"Thank *you* for saving the Hathaways' station wagon," Mrs. Bobbsey said gratefully.

The twins watched eagerly as the flaming brush was reduced to smoldering embers.

As the firemen were about to leave, Nan glanced out on the pond. In the middle of it she saw two boys in a boat. "Oh, look!" she exclaimed. "They're Danny and George!"

Bert called as loudly as he could, "Hi, Danny! Hi, George!"

The boys in the boat stood up and waved their arms. Then suddenly they seemed to sink through the bottom of the craft.

"They're up to some trick," Nan suggested.

But Danny and George began to cry out in fright.

"I think they're in trouble, Mother," Bert said.

"Can't Danny swim?" Freddie asked.

"Yes," Bert replied. "But something's gone wrong!"

Now the boys' heads disappeared under the water. As they bobbed to the surface again, the Bobbseys heard frantic cries of "Help! Help!"

Chief Holt turned to his men. "Bring up the rescue boat!" he ordered. "Freddie had a good hunch!"

Two firemen quickly uncoupled the trailer from the back of the truck and pulled it to the shore. The boat, which had an outboard motor, slid down into the water. The firemen jumped in and started off.

Meanwhile Danny and George were thrashing about wildly in the water. "Oh dear!" Nan wailed. "I hope the firemen reach them in time!"

CHAPTER XVII

THE HIDING PLACE

AS THE Bobbseys watched anxiously, the rescue boat sped across the pond. In a few minutes the firemen reached Danny and George.

They hauled the boys out of the water, then turned back. When the bow touched the shore Danny and George stepped out, dripping wet and crestfallen.

"Do you know that all of Plymouth has been looking for you?" Mrs. Bobbsey asked them.

George replied that they were unaware of this. "We were only camping out for a few days," he said.

"Did you tell your parents you were going?" the chief questioned.

George admitted that they had run off after exploding a torpedo in the basement of the Rench home. The boy glanced ruefully at Danny.

"Don't look at me like that," Danny said. "It was your idea to set off that torpedo."

"But not in our basement!" George complained.

"Where is your camping equipment?" Bert spoke up.

"Right over there," George said, pointing to some bushes near the shore. He went over and returned with two sleeping bags and a knapsack.

"I'll take these runaways home right away, Mrs. Bobbsey," the chief offered.

"Please wait a minute," Bert said. "I'd like to ask them a few more questions to clear up a mystery."

"Go ahead."

Bert looked straight at Danny. "Did you and George stay at Peacedale Village overnight?"

Danny's mouth dropped open in surprise. "Yes, we did. How did you know?"

"Flossie found your black notebook," Bert told him.

"Which led us to Billington Sea," Nan added.

Danny and George looked at each other in amazement. "But it was written in—" Danny began.

"Code," Bert finished the sentence. "And in invisible ink, too."

Danny was so surprised that he could say nothing. He merely hung his head as Bert went on, "You set off the torpedo on the Cranberry Railroad track too."

Danny nodded meekly.

"And you took the fusees," Nan said.

"No, I didn't!" Danny protested.

"Then what was that red thing I saw in your suitcase?" Bert demanded.

"That was the pen for writing in invisible ink," the boy said.

At this point the fire chief spoke in a stern voice. "Do you know who took the fusees?"

Danny answered promptly. "The man with the black bag," he said.

The Bobbseys felt certain that Danny was telling the truth. "I'm glad you didn't take them, Danny," Mrs. Bobbsey said. "They're very dangerous in the hands of children."

The chief excused himself, saying he was going to send a radio message. He strode to his car and spoke into a microphone. Returning in a few minutes, Chief Holt informed Mrs. Bobbsey that the police would notify the parents of both boys that they were safe.

"Is my mother in Plymouth?" Danny asked.

"She arrived a few hours ago," the chief explained, "and will be waiting for you at the Renchs' home."

Danny looked furtively about, as if wishing he could dash off again.

"Come on now, no more shenanigans," the fire chief said. "Hop into my car. We're ready to leave."

After the Bobbseys had thanked Chief Holt and his men, the fire fighters manned the apparatus and drove toward Plymouth.

"Well, that solves one part of the mystery," Bert said as the Bobbseys climbed into the station wagon.

When the twins returned to North Street, they excitedly told Aunt Nan what had happened.

"Poor Danny," Nan Bobbsey said. "I wouldn't want to be in his shoes right now."

"Serves him right," Bert said.

"Do you suppose his mother will let him see the Pilgrim Progress tomorrow?" Freddie asked.

"He'll make faces at us," Flossie said. "And I might laugh."

"Don't worry about that now," Aunt Nan advised. Then she added, "You all must be hungry after your trip. Supper is waiting."

After the delicious meal, Bert and Nan went next door to tell the Hathaways the good news about Danny and George.

"And we have some good news for you, too," Jack said, grinning.

"What's that?" Bert asked.

"Remember the tunnel at Saquish Head?"

"You bet."

"We're going to explore it tomorrow!"

"Great!" Bert exclaimed. "But we'll need a motorboat."

The Hathaways told them that Mary Jo and her mother had come back to Plymouth while the Bobbseys were at Billington Sea. They had proposed the trip.

"Mrs. Woodson will call for us tomorrow," Jack said.

Bert and Nan raced to tell their mother the exciting plans. "Is it all right?" Nan asked.

"If Mrs. Woodson and Mary Jo go with you. I think I'll stay here with Aunt Nan," Mrs. Bobbsey said, smiling. "With all this detective work, we really haven't had time to visit."

As usually was the case, Freddie and Flossie went to bed before Bert and Nan. "I'm too excited to sleep, anyhow," Nan said to Bert. "Come on, let's take a walk and buy some picture postcards to send Daddy, Dinah, and Sam. Is it all right, Mother?"

When Mrs. Bobbsey said yes, the twins went out to Main Street and turned left. They had noticed a large stationery and toy store next to a public telephone booth.

Bert and Nan went inside and purchased

some brightly colored picture postcards showing scenes in Plymouth. After leaving the store,
the twins lingered in front of the window to
look at the toys on display.

As they admired a model of the Old Fort,
Bert noticed a man enter the adjacent telephone
booth. He dialed a number and the boy could
not help hearing him say, "Cracky, I've got a
big deal!"

Bert's pulse quickened. He nudged Nan.
"Listen," he whispered.

Pretending to look at the other toys in the
window, the twins edged closer to the booth.
They did not risk a direct look at the man, who
might recognize them.

"I tell you it's a cinch," the fellow went on.
"A dealer in New York will take all you can
get from the Warren house!" He paused a few
seconds, then said, "Good. Okay. So long!"

The door of the phone booth folded open, and
the caller stepped out. As he stopped to light a
cigarette, Bert and Nan noticed he had a thin
face and wore a small black mustache. Without
glancing their way, he hurried off.

The twins looked about for a policeman, but
none was in sight. "Anyway," Bert said, "cap-
turing this man might alert Cracky and Lanky."

"But," said Nan, "we ought to tell the police
about the Warren house."

The boy stepped into the telephone booth and dialed police headquarters. When the lieutenant in charge heard Bert's report he thanked him and said, "We had intended to post one man at the Warrens'. Now we'll assign three officers to that place."

Bert and Nan found it hard to fall asleep that night. So much was due to happen next day—the search at Saquish Head, the Pilgrim Progress parade, and the trap which the police were setting for Lanky and Cracky.

Early next morning the doorbell rang. Flossie jumped up from the breakfast table to answer it. Mary Jo stood there.

"Oh, you're up with the worms!" The little twin giggled as Mary Jo entered.

"You mean I'm an early bird?"

"That's right," Flossie said, dimpling.

Soon the twins were ready to go. They had donned swim suits and sport shirts. Like Mary Jo, they were barefoot.

"Be careful," their mother warned them. "Freddie and Flossie, stay close to Mrs. Woodson."

"We will, we will," they chorused.

"When will you come back, Mary Jo?" Mrs. Bobbsey asked.

"About noontime. 'By."

As the children trooped out of the house,

Jack and Jane joined them. Together they hurried to the town dock, where Mrs. Woodson was
waiting. "Here we go for another big adventure," she said, smiling.

When they reached Saquish, Jack and Bert
hopped onto the small dock and tied up the
boat.

"Come on, let's explore the tunnel right
away," Bert suggested.

"Okay, let's go!" Jane said, her eyes sparkling
with excitement.

Mrs. Woodson offered to play with Freddie
and Flossie on the beach while the others examined the ruins of old Fort Standish.

"See you later, Mother," Mary Jo said. She
quickly led the others to the spot where Nan
had fallen into the pit.

Bert pulled a small flashlight from his shirt
pocket.

"We're prepared this time," he announced as
he removed his shirt and lowered himself into
the hole.

Nan did likewise, followed by Mary Jo,
Jane, and Jack.

Bert beamed his light along the dark passage.
"Wow! It's really spooky in here," he said.

The walls were lined with red brick. Water
oozed from them and dripped from the ceiling.

"Here's the pool," Bert said. "Say, what

were we worried about? It's only ten feet across."

"It's not dangerous at all," Nan said. "We can swim to the other side."

With Bert leading the way, the explorers soon swam to the other side of the pool. They progressed farther into the tunnel.

"It takes a bend down here," Bert said, cautiously stepping over the spongy floor of the hidden passageway. Suddenly he stopped and whistled. "Look, it branches off into three other tunnels! Which one shall we explore first?"

"The one to the left," Nan suggested.

"Okay."

"Boy, is it ever cool down here!" Jack said.

"It's too clammy for me," Jane remarked with a shudder.

All at once the beam of Bert's light picked up a low doorway. "I wonder what's in there," he said. Bert bent down and flashed the light inside. "Wow! Look here!"

The boy stepped through the doorway and the others followed. They were in a small room. On the floor lay a pile of antique silver and wooden pieces.

"This is the thieves' hideout!" Nan declared.

"What a discovery!" Jack exclaimed.

The children stopped to examine the pewter pitcher and a pair of silver candlesticks. They

"This is the thieves' hideout," Nan declared

were in good condition, as were an antique Pilgrim crib and other museum pieces.

When they finished examining the loot, Jane said, "Suppose Cracky and Lanky come back and find us here."

"Mother will warn us," Mary Jo assured her.

"But suppose the thieves have a secret entrance to the tunnel and your mother doesn't see them?"

"Jane has a good point," Bert said. "Let's carry these things out right away."

The children picked up all they could carry. With Bert leading the way, they headed back in the direction from which they had come.

When he came to the three-forked tunnels, Bert paused. "Where do we go from here?"

"I think we turn left," Nan said.

"No, right," Jack insisted.

"Seems to me it was the middle passage," Bert said.

In the gloom and darkness it was hard to remember just how they had come. Bert cast his light on the floor of the tunnel in search of footprints.

"Willikers!" Jack burst out. "There are footprints in each of the passages!"

"Let's follow the middle one first," Bert suggested.

As he led the way, the children, burdened

with the antiques, followed along the dripping tunnel.

Presently Bert stopped. "Listen!"

In the distance the children could hear the pounding of the waves on the shore.

"This isn't the way we came! It must be a secret exit," Bert exclaimed. "Let's see where it goes."

But as he hurried forward, the boy suddenly stopped in his tracks again. Water gushed through the tunnel. In seconds it was knee-deep!

CHAPTER XVIII

HAPPY PILGRIMS

ALL the children recognized their danger immediately. The tide was coming in. They might be trapped by the rising water!

"Hurry!" Jane urged, as they sloshed along.

"Yes," Jack said worriedly. "The tide rises fast here. If we don't get out soon—"

Bert passed the flashlight to Jack, who had been in the lead since the children turned around. "Faster!" he urged.

The five explorers splashed through the rising tide. Presently they came to the three forks.

"Now which one?" Jack asked. He paused to cast his flashlight beam about.

As they pondered, small voices sounded faintly in the distance.

"Someone's calling us!" Jane whispered.

"It's Freddie and Flossie!" Bert said. "They must be yelling down into the hole."

"Here we come!" Nan shouted back.

After listening carefully for a few moments, Mary Jo said, "It's the right fork. That's where the voices are coming from."

The others agreed.

"Hurray for Freddie and Flossie!" Jack cried out as they hurried along the tunnel.

When they came to the pit of water Jack handed the pewter pitcher he was carrying to Jane. Then he swam across. Reaching the other side, he said, "Toss me the things."

The others did as he suggested and soon the pile of loot was on the other side of the pool. Then Jane, Mary Jo, Bert, and Nan made their way across.

Soon they came to the opening. Looking up, they saw the small twins peering down.

"Thanks for calling us," Bert said. He stood on Jack's shoulders and climbed out. Then he reached down to help the girls up. As Jack passed the stolen articles to Bert, Mrs. Woodson hurried over to see what was happening.

"Goodness gracious!" she said. "What did you find?"

"The things that Lanky and Cracky stole," Bert said, hauling Jack to the surface.

Quickly the children loaded the articles into the boat.

"We'll take them to the Plymouth police,"

Mrs. Woodson said. "I certainly am proud of you."

After everyone had stepped aboard, Mrs. Woodson started the motor and they skimmed across Plymouth Harbor.

"We're like pirates in reverse," Bert joked as they neared the town dock.

"Oh, Mack!" Jack called out. "See what we have here!"

The harbor master hastened down the ramp to meet them. He was amazed to see the loot. Then he grinned. "Won't Lanky and Cracky be surprised when they return to the tunnel?"

"If they ever do get back!" Bert said with a wink.

The children helped to carry the stolen articles to Mack's car. "I'll take them to the police station right away," he offered.

Waving good-by, Mary Jo and her mother went off in the motorboat. Bert, Nan, and the Hathaways hurried home to tell of their exciting discovery.

"Now if the police can only catch those thieves during the Progress!" Aunt Nan said. She was as excited as the young folks.

After lunch Freddie and Flossie could not hold down their energy. "Let's practice for the parade," the little boy suggested.

Aunt Nan Shaw said this was a good idea.

She and Mrs. Bobbsey took the twins to the basement of the church near the foot of Leyden Street.

As Aunt Nan opened the door to the big room the children gasped in amazement. Row after row of costumes hung on racks.

"Oh, what lovely dresses!" Nan exclaimed, as she hurried over to examine the Pilgrim outfits.

"They're just like the ones the Pilgrims wore," Miss Shaw explained.

"Oh, may we wear anything we like for our own little parade?" Flossie asked.

"I suggest," said Aunt Nan, "that you choose something from that last rack. Those are old costumes and won't be used today."

Giggling among themselves, the twins went off and spent several minutes making their choices. Then they pulled them on over their clothes.

"All ready!" Bert announced.

Nan and Flossie appeared first, looking charming in colorful cotton dresses with wide white collars and aprons. Bert followed, dressed as a Pilgrim soldier and carrying a musket. Freddie, last, carried a drum.

"The drum's almost as big as you are, Freddie," Aunt Nan said, chuckling.

She put a Pilgrim baby doll into Flossie's arms and presented Nan with a hymn book.

"The four of you could have stepped right out of 1620," Miss Shaw said, beaming.

Flossie rocked the doll in her arms while Nan held the hymn book tightly in the crook of her elbow.

"Come on, let's march," Freddie said impatiently.

They all walked up the basement steps and outside the church with drummer Freddie in the lead, followed by soldier Bert, Nan, and Flossie. The Bobbseys marched up and down to the beat of the drum.

As sightseers looked on, smiling, Flossie said, "Isn't this fun!" and the others agreed.

Presently Mrs. Bobbsey felt they had practiced enough, so the children returned to the basement of the church and took off their Pilgrim clothes.

"You'll have to report back promptly at four o'clock," Aunt Nan told them, "to take part in the Progress."

When the hour came for the big event, about fifty people congregated at the church. What a busy time it was as committee women assisted children and grownups into their costumes!

Again the Bobbsey twins were told about the parts they would take in the Progress. The girls were to represent Mary and Remember Allerton. Freddie would be Henry Sampson, and Bert would march as Richard More.

"I'd rather be the drummer!" Freddie declared.

Aunt Nan explained that Freddie was not old enough to play the role of the drummer.

"Everything must be as nearly like the original Pilgrim Progress as possible," Miss Shaw said.

Freddie was satisfied, and he grinned as his collar was straightened by a lovely dark-haired woman on the committee.

"We're so delighted to have you Bobbseys with us today," said the woman, whom Aunt Nan introduced as Miss Crosby. "I know you'll be a wonderful addition to our Progress."

Mary Allerton and her sister Remember curtsied at the compliments and Henry Sampson and Richard More bowed politely.

"Everybody outside!" Miss Crosby said, and the "Pilgrims" assembled in front of the church. Aunt Nan saw that each one took his proper place in line.

Behind the drummer came Elder Brewster, Governor Bradford, and Miles Standish, three abreast. Following them were the rest of the Plymouth Colony, singly and in pairs.

Rat-tat-tat! Rat-tat-tat! went the drum as the

The parade started up Leyden Street

parade started up Leyden Street. When it reached Main Street, the drummer paused and beat out a roll. Hundreds of onlookers had lined both sides of the street to watch the solemn procession.

The "Pilgrims" marched up the hill to the front of the old church where they stopped again. Then the party proceeded up the granite steps to Burial Hill. The path was flanked with ancient tombstones.

Nan gazed over the harbor toward the lighthouse. She sighed as she thought of the Pilgrim Fathers. They had looked out across the same harbor many years before.

Now the Pilgrims formed a circle on the brow of the hill. Elder Brewster delivered a short sermon as everyone listened intently. Hymns were sung by the congregation.

When the service was over, the drummer started back down the long flight of stone steps. The marchers filed past the old church and down Leyden Street. As Bert marched, he wondered whether the police trap had worked. Had Lanky and Cracky been captured?

On reaching the starting point, the young people in the parade began chatting gaily with the Bobbseys. "How did you like it?" asked a blond-haired girl. She represented Priscilla Mullins, a Pilgrim maid.

"It was wonderful," Nan replied. "I'll never forget it as long as I live."

Just then Jane and Jack rushed up. "You all were wonderful!" Jane exclaimed.

"Everyone acted super!" Jack said, grinning. "You're real Pilgrims!"

"Thanks," Bert said as he removed his tall black hat.

Once they had taken off their costumes, the Bobbseys and their friends hurried outside.

"I wonder—" Bert began, when suddenly he was interrupted by the sound of a police siren. A squad car pulled up alongside the children.

"Are you the Bobbsey twins?" the driver asked.

"Yes, sir," Bert replied.

The officer smiled. "I have good news for you."

"Did you catch Lanky and Cracky?" Nan cried.

"Yes," the policeman replied, "and their friend with the black mustache."

"Oh boy!" Freddie shouted. Flossie clapped her hands and beamed.

"They were taking some things from the Warren house when three of our plainclothesmen snapped handcuffs on them," the policeman continued. "Stealing antiques is a new racket of theirs."

"And their last one, too, I hope!" Bert said, grinning.

The policeman thanked the Bobbseys for their help and drove off as Mrs. Bobbsey and Aunt Nan located the twins. They rushed up and hugged the children.

"Such excitement," Mrs. Bobbsey said. "Wait until Daddy hears about your latest mystery!"

"Hurrah! Hurrah! We've caught the ghost of Clark's Island!" Jack said.

"I had a hunch you would," Aunt Nan declared proudly as they walked home.

The Bobbseys had been in the house only five minutes when the doorbell rang. Flossie went to answer it. Mr. Warren stepped inside, his face wreathed with smiles.

"I hear you helped catch the ghost!" he said.

As all the children began to talk at once, Mr. Warren went on, "I have some important information to tell you."

"What is it?" Bert asked eagerly.

"We finally received consent today to open the secret drawer in the old desk."

"Did you find a secret in it?" Flossie bubbled.

"Indeed we did. And what a find it was! We have you twins to thank for discovering the secret drawer."

Mr. Warren said a miniature model of an old ship was secreted inside the drawer. "She's a beauty and is supposed to look like the 'Mayflower,' even to the rigging and forecastle!"

The twins were thrilled, and Nan declared it made their stay in Plymouth "extra perfect."

After Mr. Warren had gone, Mrs. Bobbsey looked at the children and said, "Yes, it has been a perfect visit with Aunt Nan. And my young Pilgrims have seen everything."

"Not everything," Freddie spoke up. "We still have to see that 'Mayflower II!' "

The others smiled and agreed. "Let's go!" said Bert.

When the BOBBSEY TWINS find a mysterious message in a tree trunk in the deep woods, they start on an exciting adventure to uncover a settler's long-lost treasure. A logrolling, a lost papoose, and the cry of "Timber!" make fun and thrills in

THE BOBBSEY TWINS' FOREST ADVENTURE